BOOKS BY KEELY BROOKE KEITH

Uncharted Christmas

KEELY BROOKE KEITH

Edenbrooke
Press

For Megan Easley-Walsh,
My fellow author
and friend across the pond

CHAPTER ONE

December 18, 2030

Dr. Lydia Bradshaw refused to believe the rumor predicting it would snow on Christmas Day. Such idealistic holiday pleasantries might be commonplace in the northern hemisphere at this time of year, but not here in the Land where the summer solstice was mere days away. Holding fast to the truth was the only way she would survive the Land's present circumstances with her professional dignity intact.

And the truth was that Christmastime in Good Springs heralded the gentle beginning of summer—a sweet time when long evenings beckoned her to slowly sip the sunset, whether she was preparing dinner for her family or riding Dapple home from house calls outside the village. Proper December weather on this hidden island in the middle of the South Atlantic Ocean brought bright sunrises, warm days with lazy strolls on the shore, and teaching little Andrew how to catch fireflies in the paddock while soft evening breezes fanned her skirts.

Not with snow flurries sticking to her eyelashes.

She brushed the uninvited snowflakes away from her face and tightened her woolen shawl as she hurried from one patient's house to the next. Frost had formed on her medical bag's handle, sticking its metal to her glove. The only frost in the Land in early December should be in the icebox in the cellar. Then again, nothing else had been normal this year, so why should she expect the weather to meet her expectations?

Perhaps the villagers' Christmas snow prediction would come true.

As she passed the chapel where her father preached on Sundays, she waved more snowflakes away from her face while following the second-born Cotter child to the next urgent call. They passed the old library, which was her favorite building in the village, then the schoolhouses, and finally the bare lot where the market bustled with traders every Saturday morning.

Daydreaming about quiet hours in the library or balmy summer days at the market tempted her constantly, but she resisted the urge to look to the right and the left. Nothing else could matter while answering the call of duty.

Her boot heels crunched the icy crystals scattered on the cobblestone street as she trailed the Cotter boy toward his parents' tidy house where she had been summoned to examine the eldest child—a girl of ten, whom the boy said was shaky and refused to leave her hiding place.

If the girl's condition was indeed what Lydia expected, this would be the third call to aid a panicked youngster so far this week.

And that, too, she blamed on the uncommon weather.

Hopefully, this patient would be easier to calm than the others. She barely had time to answer this call for help before her three o'clock obstetrics appointment at the Foster farm, and her reputation disallowed tardiness, no matter that the scheduled patient was her younger sister.

The frigid wind whipped at her bonnet, flipping its starched rim up and down like a storm-tossed wave. She shouldn't have stored her winter wardrobe already. Since the sun still shone most days—albeit not as early nor as late as it should because of the ring of haze that darkened the horizon—she held hope for the Land to have a summer this year.

Even though the spring weather hadn't been normal, the few hours of daily sunlight that pierced the volcanic ash in the earth's upper atmosphere had thawed the soil after the harshest winter the Land had ever known.

If only the frost that smothered her spirit would likewise thaw.

No! She could not succumb to the dread and complaining that had taken over many of the villagers' attitudes. It would be Christmas soon, and no one deserved a discontented wife or mother at what was supposed to be the most joyous time of year, especially her Connor and her Andrew.

She had seen worse situations than out-of-season snow. She could fight this unrelenting melancholy. By the increase in patient calls, it was safe to assume she wasn't the only soul struggling to stay positive. Probably the entire world was presently downcast.

Connor said the volcanic ash layer surrounding the globe would have darkened the rest of the planet much worse than what the Land was experiencing. The atmospheric anomaly that helped to hide the Land was somehow keeping their skies clear directly above. He said that meant the unbroken cloud cover the rest of the world was enduring would have cooled the continents more than the Land.

If she could trust anyone's opinion on what was happening, it was Connor's. Not only was the former Unified States Naval Aviator the Land's first outsider since the Founders arrived here in the 1860s, he was also the Land's most ardent protector... and her husband.

If Connor said life was better in the Land—even with the haze on the horizon that shortened and cooled the days—it was true. Those poor souls of the outside world must be terribly miserable. And also the doctors who tended to them. Lydia only had to bear a late-spring snow and more requests for house calls than usual.

Many, many more requests for house calls.

Not all Lydia's patients were afflicted in the same manner, but she was seeing a pattern. The calls for help weren't the usual medical emergencies she used to encounter. No broken bones to set or deep lacerations to stitch.

These days, the cries were frantic, yet the symptoms benign. Half the older folks in the village suffered from a deep sadness that amplified their every ache, and the adolescents' anxious spirits deprived them of logic and sleep.

Another pattern was emerging too: it seemed each young married woman in the village was pregnant.

All the young married women except her.

That didn't matter now. Couldn't matter now. She and Connor had been blessed with Andrew. Her precious boy would turn three at the end of the month, and he filled the Colburn house with the energy of a dozen children.

That should be enough to satisfy her maternal longings.

Besides, at present she could hardly find time for every patient who sent for her. She had experienced pregnancy once and remembered how difficult it had been to tend to half the patients she had now.

So her inability to conceive again was probably a blessing. Yes, that was it. A blessing.

And one must always count their blessings. Hadn't her mother frequently said so? Her sweet, departed mother, who had been blessed with five children, a peaceful home, and the time to decorate the house for Christmas every year.

If she could see Lydia's performance as a wife and mother and the house so void of Christmas cheer, she would probably be dreadfully disappointed in her.

No, Hannah Colburn wasn't easily disappointed.

Once again, Lydia couldn't do anything as graciously as her mother had.

Lydia's elder sisters, Adeline and Maggie, were both models of domestic efficiency with their big families and beautiful homes. Even Mandy could patiently tend to baby Will while being six months along with her and Levi's second child, and she still found time to teach music lessons, craft new instruments to trade, and have a hot meal on the table and a smile on her face when Levi came home each day.

At least, that was how Lydia imagined her sister-in-law's daily life.

Her heels sank into the slushy soil as she stepped from the road to the Cotter family's front gate. The boy had already charged ahead of her and past Mrs. Cotter, who was standing inside the open front door with one arm holding her toddler on her hip and the other hand rubbing her pregnant belly.

"Thank you for coming, Dr. Bradshaw," the woman declared before Lydia had ascended the porch steps. "Grace is curled up in the corner. She was trembling frightfully earlier but has stopped now. I don't think she's ill exactly, though something is wrong with her. Harold is working at the mill until sundown. I didn't know what to do, so I sent Billy to fetch you."

"That is always best in these situations, Mrs. Cotter." Lydia stepped from the snowy porch into the cozy entryway, her cold nose soothed by the aroma of bread baking. Freshly woven pine garland swirled around the banister of the polished staircase ahead of her. To her left, steam rose from the pots on the stove, and to her right, a fire glowed in the hearth. "Where is Grace now?"

Mrs. Cotter's hospitable hands awaited Lydia's icy shawl and frozen spring bonnet. Melting snow drips tinked on the clean floorboards while Mrs. Cotter hung the items on a coat tree. "She's in the parlor, just through here."

Lydia wiped her boots on the entryway rug and followed Mrs. Cotter through a short hallway into a beautifully arranged parlor. More garland outlined an organized bookcase. Two armchairs, each cradling needlepoint pillows sporting festive Christmas designs, flanked a plush divan. A crocheted blanket made of Christmas-colored yarn covered the back of the divan like an invitation to nestle in and read awhile.

Lydia had unboxed none of her family's Christmas decorations, and she certainly hadn't read for pleasure in a long time.

Mrs. Cotter caught Lydia's eye and pointed to the corner behind the second armchair. Another child ran to Mrs. Cotter from the kitchen and furled his arms around her aproned waist. "I finished writing my alphabet, Mama. Read me a story now, please."

"In a few minutes, baby. Dr. Bradshaw is here to see Grace."

Billy darted into the parlor behind his little brother, his face still flushed from the cold outside. "May I have a biscuit, Mama?"

"Not yet, Billy." She looked down at her daughter, who was ignoring them all. "Gracie, Dr. Bradshaw is here to see you."

The girl didn't respond.

"Gracie, sweetie, Dr. Bradshaw came all this way for you. Please, come out."

When her daughter's position still didn't change, Mrs. Cotter looked at Lydia with a concerned brow and lifted an uncertain hand. "Grace stared out the window all morning after her father left for the mill. When the snow started falling, she got herself in a tizzy and hid back there. I wasn't worried till I noticed she was shaking and such. She's never behaved like this. Can you help her, Doctor?"

Before Lydia could answer, the boys both fired questions at their mother, pulling at her apron and begging for attention and biscuits.

Lydia gave the girl a quick study. This was not a medical emergency, nor had she expected it to be. Still, duty bound her to answer any call. That used to mean putting her safety at risk by rushing to save others; now her job had simmered to more frequent but less sensational heroics.

She set her medical bag on the floor beside the sofa and dropped her cold gloves atop it. The girl peeked one eye open. Lydia slid the armchair away, opening the hiding place wide enough for two. "Hello, Grace. Mind if I join you back there?"

The girl gazed up at Lydia with wet eyes and a quivering bottom lip.

Lydia had seen that look on other young faces since the haze filled the horizon eight months ago. She offered Mrs. Cotter a reassuring smile. "Would you take your sons to the kitchen while Grace and I have a chat?"

"Yes, of course." Mrs. Cotter caught her sons' hands. "Come now, Tommy, Billy."

Lydia lowered herself to the floor beside the girl and spread her damp skirt hem. Heat from the gray leaf log in the fireplace warmed the room all the way to its edges. She leaned her palms against the rug behind her as she gazed about the parlor. "This is a lovely hiding place you have here. I can see why you chose it. It's safe and warm."

Out of the corner of her eye, she could see Grace watching her. She gave pause for the girl to speak, but when she didn't, Lydia continued in a relaxed voice. "Yes, I would tuck myself away in this room too, especially on cold days that shouldn't be cold. And definitely on days when the grown-ups spoke of clouds and snow and not knowing what would come of the crops and the livestock and the village."

Grace unlocked her arms from around her knobby knees long enough to wipe her nose on her sleeve. Lydia withdrew a fresh handkerchief from her dress pocket and offered it to her. "Your mother is worried about you. She sent for me to make sure you aren't ill. I don't think you are ill. Do you?"

Grace accepted the handkerchief and shook her head.

It wasn't the vocal response Lydia was hoping for, but it was a start. "I've been out in that weather all day, going from house to house to help patients." She held out a hand. "Do my fingers feel cold to you?"

Grace felt Lydia's hand, unaware it was her temperature that was being checked. Her voice cracked from a tear-filled afternoon. "Maybe a little."

"Your fingers are a little cool as well." She felt the girl's forehead and neck. "You don't have a fever, nor are your glands swollen."

"I wanted to tell Mama I wasn't sick, but I couldn't talk."

"Why couldn't you talk?"

"I was too upset, I guess."

"Big emotions and no idea what to do with them." Lydia brushed the girl's hair out of her eyes. "I know what that's like."

"You do?"

"Of course. But you must understand it isn't a condition you should try to keep. Your body wants to return to its normal state. It's trying to do what God designed it to do. You must let it." Lydia widened her eyes like she had an idea. That always got Andrew's attention. "Why, I have just the thing to get you back on your feet!"

"What is it?"

She stood and took her patient's hand. "It's in my bag over here." She skirted the armchair and sat on the divan, then patted the cushion beside her.

Grace sat too and tried to peer into the medical bag while Lydia rummaged in a side pocket.

Lydia gave her a sly smile. "Now, now. Mustn't peek. This is where I keep all my best remedies."

The girl crinkled her nose. "I don't want to take medicine."

"And I don't believe you need any medicine. I'll listen to your lungs and your heart to assure your mother, of course, but I think there is a whole different remedy for your distress." She withdrew a wax paper packet filled with soft candy. "My cousin's wife makes the most delicious caramel chews."

She opened the packet wide enough for the girl to reach inside. Grace's fingers had lost most of their tremble. She needed someone—anyone with a confident hand and full attention—to snap her out of the lies that had gripped her mind.

Only one who had fallen into that pit before would know how to help someone else out.

While the girl concentrated on chewing the thick candy, Lydia spoke about the slow, sweet-smelling process of making the delicious caramel. She listened to her patient's strong heart and clear lungs during deliberate pauses.

After a quick look into Grace's eyes and a check of her reflexes, she closed her medical bag. "Just as I suspected, Grace, you are in fine health. Is that what you suspected too?"

The girl nodded, then swallowed her caramel and began cleaning her teeth with her tongue. "So, what's wrong with me?"

Lydia retied Grace's loose hair bow. "It's the same condition that currently afflicts many other young people right now. It is fear. For the past few months, you've heard adults speak of frightening things no one in the Land has ever considered. Now you see snow when it should be warm outside, and you think of all the scary possibilities. When we dwell on such things, our bodies follow our minds."

The girl's gaze darted to the window then back to Lydia. "Dr. Bradshaw, I don't want to freeze to death."

"You won't. But you can't spend your life hiding by the fireplace, either."

"I don't want my brothers to die or the baby when it comes. Or Father. He has to walk to work in the cold. It makes me so scared. Then I shake and all I can think about is how scared I am."

"But your father is fine and your brothers are safe and the baby is the warm inside your mother's tummy, right?"

"Well... I guess so."

"Since no one is in any danger of dying, whenever your feelings get so big you tremble and want to hide, that is your signal to become a special inspector."

"A what?"

"A special inspector. Just like in the old storybooks, you must look for clues to what is really happening."

"What clues?"

"Truth clues. Are you safe and warm and healthy?"

"Yes."

"That's the truth. Always look for the truth." She waved a hand about the room. "The weather is colder than normal right now, but are you warm in your house?"

"Yes."

"Do you have all the food you need?"

"Yes."

"Even though the adults have new challenges to face and they discuss matters in worried tones, are they still taking care of you and your brothers?"

"Yes."

Lydia lifted a dramatic finger. "Those are some clues to the truth. The Bible tells us to think on things that are true, and this, my dear, is why. So, instead of letting your mind tie your body into knots, use that energy to search out the truth. Understand?"

Grace nodded, then pointed to Lydia's medical bag. "May I have one more of those candies? Not for myself, but for Mama? I think I might have scared her too."

That brought warmth to Lydia's heart. She checked the wristwatch Connor had given her on her last birthday. "Perhaps your mother will get a candy after her next medical exam, but for now, I must hurry to another patient's home."

* * *

Philip Roberts looped a thumb through his dinner jacket's buttonhole as he surveyed the bustling dining hall. Never was the Inn at Falls Creek quite so alive as when it pulsed with an eager supper crowd. Who could be lonely in a place known for elevating the spirits of weary travelers and lifting the gloom of cold nights?

While inhaling the savory aromas of Sybil's cooking, Philip watched the sufferings of long wagon rides or bone-chilling outdoor labor melt away from the inn's hungry guests. More than once, he too had forgotten his own discomforts while in this fellowship of new friends, delicious food, and warm firelight.

No matter how alluring the scents of seasoned trout and vegetables, freshly baked bread, and cinnamon cooked apples were, he wasn't here for his own sake, but for theirs—the residents and guests of Falls Creek.

Pastoring the only church in this isolated region of the Land meant encouraging many a road-worn traveler to carry on, whatever their journey might be. Yet lately, he found his greatest endeavor to be furtively checking the ever-changing rotation of faces for the one person he prayed would stay here forever.

Only he didn't know her name.

Nor what she looked like.

He simply knew the Lord had prepared one special woman to complement his earthly existence and to share the work of his life's calling. One woman he could spend a lifetime adoring, nourishing and cherishing, loving as Christ loves the Church.

And he believed this dining hall was where he would someday find her.

Tonight, however, his secret endeavor was unnecessary. He already knew every face in the dining hall. He'd made acquaintance with the traders and travelers who were only staying a night or two, and he'd lived in the parsonage across the road long enough to consider the inn's permanent residents his friends.

And every woman living here already had found her perfect match.

Tonight's meal would be a simple dinner, or so he'd thought. But a short counseling session at the chapel had made him tardy for dinner, and now all the seats at his usual table were taken. He scanned the rest of the tables for an empty chair, but found none. Waiting in the doorway would be distasteful, so he removed himself to the corridor.

Eva, the inn's manager, carried a full plate in each hand as she swirled from the kitchen to the dining hall. Her sister, Sybil, was behind her with two water pitchers, waddling slowly to accommodate her full-term pregnancy. Though Eva had long ago accepted Philip as Falls Creek's overseer and had invited him to eat at the inn daily, when the ladies were this busy, he thought it best to wait in the parlor until the rush had passed.

As he stepped from the corridor's shadow to the parlor's gracious light, the joyful chatter in the dining hall didn't wane. His stomach growled, still indignant that he'd missed lunch. It was easy to do when he was in such deep study of the Scripture and communion with God that he lost track of time.

The flesh cared not of the hour, and now he was famished.

He could go back to the parsonage and make a meal of the hunk of bread and dried apricots he was saving for breakfast. But, since Eva had spotted him, she might think it odd of him to leave without eating.

He glanced across the corridor and down to the open kitchen doorway, wishing he could go in there and find his own dinner. If he had a wife who worked at the inn, it would make sense for him to walk into the kitchen, fill a plate, and eat at the little side table when there was no room in the dining hall.

As it was, he didn't feel entitled to being fed three meals a day here, let alone help himself to the kitchen's bounty. Though he preached the Sunday sermons, maintained the chapel, and helped Isaac in the fields or Solo in the stables when there were no travelers swapping work for room and board, he still felt like a visitor here. Regardless of how kind Sybil was, he could never set foot in her kitchen without being invited.

But if he were married to a lady who worked here, he could stride into the kitchen any time he liked, just as the other husbands did. Simply having one's wife in a room seemed to give the husband validation to enter it. A husband's entrance needn't be explained when his very presence announced: *I'm here because my wife is here.*

But Philip had no wife, despite years of midnight prayers.

While Philip mindlessly perused the dusty volumes that filled the parlor's neglected bookcase, two traders ambled out of the dining hall. They both had toothpicks between their lips and rubbed their full bellies. They gave Philip a polite nod on their way to the inn's broad front door.

When it shut behind them, Philip backed away from the bookcase to check their empty seats in the dining hall. Eva was collecting the dirty dishes and had yet to wipe the table. He dare not rush her.

The parlor's stuffed sofa seemed too regal a place for a single man to sit alone, so he selected an armchair near the crackling fire. Before he sat, a thunderous knock shook the front door. Usually, after guests had arranged their accommodations with Eva, they didn't knock as they came and went from the inn to the stables or bunkhouse or shower house.

The caller must be a new arrival.

Since Eva was busy, Philip answered the door. Frosty wind whistled into the parlor, swirling snow over his polished dress shoes. Across the threshold stood a broad-shouldered man with desperate eyes, an ice-flecked hat, and a weeks' worth of beard growth. Behind him two bleary-eyed women shivered, one of average height, one short enough even Philip felt tall. Something about the petite young lady seeming achingly familiar.

Philip swung the door wide. "Do come in. Terribly cold tonight. Are you all well?"

The three stepped inside and only inched far enough onto the mat for Philip to shut the door behind them. The fellow pulled off one icy glove and thrust his hand out to shake Philip's. "Noah Vestal."

"Philip Roberts. Pleased to meet you."

"My sisters and I are traveling to Good Springs and need a room."

"Of course, of course." Philip backed away from the door and peered into the dining hall. "The inn's staff is busy serving supper at present." He opened his hand to the plush sofa that wasn't his to offer. "Please, sit down while I alert the manager for you."

The taller of the two ladies stepped forward, breaking the trance of her shivering companion. "Actually, we've been riding in the wagon all day. My sister and I are desperate for the washroom."

Philip pointed across the corridor. "Yes, of course. Through there."

The women hurried away with scuttling steps. The petite woman met Philip's gaze as she passed him, her hazel eyes tawny against her glassy skin. If he'd met her before, he would have remembered those eyes.

Noah Vestal took off his other glove, but stayed on the front rug. "Sorry for arriving without a reservation."

"It's not my place to pardon you, sir, nor to make reservations. I'm but the village overseer." He glanced at the window, which would have given a view of the chapel in clear weather. "I do believe Eva is accustomed to receiving guests without notice."

"Eva?"

"The inn's manager."

The instant he spoke her name, Eva breezed into the room, her hair pulled tightly back, her arms stacked with dirty plates. "Mr. Roberts, have you brought some company this evening?"

Her beauty and boldness would have made most men blush. Not Philip. "Eva, this is Mr. Noah Vestal. He and his sisters need accommodation for the evening."

Eva looked behind the men at the front door. "Sisters?"

Noah lifted his whiskered chin at the corridor and melting ice pellets dripped from his hat. "They're using your washroom."

Eva nodded. "Ah." She flicked a glance at Philip. "Sybil made you a plate in the kitchen. Go on in. Here." She held out the stack of plates. "Mind taking these to the sink while I attend to Mr. Vestal?"

"Don't mind at all."

As he left the parlor with the armload of dishes, Eva asked Noah what he could trade for a room and how long he wished to stay.

"A week, if possible. The journey has been harder on my sisters than we expected. They need a rest, as do the horses."

The dishes wet Philip's hands as he walked the corridor to the kitchen. Ladies' voices murmured inside the washroom. Were they talking about him? Had they noticed him at all?

The latent boyishness that had been dormant for two decades tempted him to try to decipher their words. He renounced the impulse at once. A man of God dare not consider immature behavior.

Sybil met him in the kitchen doorway, her cheeks pink, her pregnant body hoisting a flour-covered apron like a ship's sail. "Is Isaac still eating in the dining hall?"

Philip set the dirty dishes by the double-basin sink. "I don't know. Shall I fetch him for you?"

She tugged her apron over her head and smiled. "No, I just wanted to join him." She picked up her plate of food from the counter top then pointed at another plate on the little table. "That's for you. Enjoy!"

"Thank you. Very kind. Smells delicious."

Alone in the stuffy kitchen, he shucked off his dinner jacket, hung it over the back of the chair, then sat to eat. The view from the private table left him relying on sounds to detect when the ladies left the washroom and joined their brother in Eva's office. They didn't close the office door, so Philip listened intently.

Eva accepted Noah's offer to trade a gallon of lamp oil for eight night's room and board for the three of them. It was a generous offer on Noah's part, and he must have known it. With an unusual beat to his speech, he negotiated for his sisters to have a private double room upstairs while he stayed out in the bunkhouse.

Only one sister spoke while they were in the office, and it was the voice of the taller one. Noah called her *Caroline*. Philip waited to hear the other sister's name, but it was never said. Eva asked where they were from and where they were traveling to.

Noah kept his answers brief, as most men do: From Northcrest. Headed to Good Springs.

When Eva offered for them to go into the dining hall for the meal, Philip stood from his chair and gripped his jacket, eager to join them. He didn't know why. Perhaps his spirit could sense they needed encouragement.

Perhaps he was simply intrigued.

Caroline declined the offer for them all, insisting they had eaten their rations before arriving and only needed baths and beds tonight.

Philip lowered himself to his seat and picked at his dinner roll. In his travels to each village while training to be an overseer, he had met the elders of Northcrest and many of the people there, but these folks hadn't been among them.

Still, he couldn't shake the sensation that he knew the youngest Vestal sibling.

Nor could he ignore the feeling that she recognized him too.

CHAPTER TWO

It was half past eleven when Lydia closed the kitchen door, shutting out the bitter winds and the dark of night. She couldn't lock out the chill of another day spent doing all the right things but feeling as though everything was wrong with her life.

Out-of-season snow melted from her boots. She removed her damp shawl and turned the dial on the oil lamp that her father always left burning on the table until the last family member was home for the night. Before she married Connor, her father would wait up for her to come home, or try to at least. Most nights, she found him dozing in his parlor chair. Not anymore. After John Colburn had passed the task of protecting Lydia to her husband, he spent his evenings upstairs in his room, sound asleep.

According to the Land's cherished traditions, it was now Connor's sacred duty to guard his wife. But he had a different upbringing in America and gave Lydia far more freedom than most women in the Land enjoyed. Whenever she worked late, he watched for her in his own way. Once their son was sleeping, Connor often went out to his workroom in the barn to tinker with his hodgepodge of electronic items from the outside world. Occasionally, when he'd had a hard day, he would go upstairs and fall asleep on top of the covers while he waited for her to come home. This evening it couldn't be the former, since she had just come from settling her horse into its stall for the night and Connor wasn't in the barn.

After the kitchen lamp's flame breathed its last, the warm glow of the ever-burning gray leaf log in the stone fireplace still provided enough light for her to make her way through the kitchen. Hours ago, her stomach had given up its growling for dinner, and now she was too tired to eat.

As she stepped through the wide doorway from the kitchen into the parlor, the firelight glowing from the two-sided fireplace cast faint shadows from one piece of well-loved furniture to the next. A dark figure stirred in the armchair by the fire.

Lydia paused at the bottom of the staircase and smiled at Connor as he opened his eyes. "Did you fall asleep in my father's chair?"

Connor closed the Bible that was resting on his lap. "It's the best chair in the house."

She leaned against the baluster, letting her tired body pause while she waited for her husband to meet her by the stairs. She didn't have to wait long. His years of military training ensured he awakened quickly, ready for anything.

He slipped his hands around her waist and drew her into his warm embrace. "Long day, Doc?"

"The longest. Eighteen hours straight. Third week in a row."

He leaned down to kiss her. "What can I do to make it better?"

She lifted her heels and met him halfway. "That."

He obliged and kissed her again. "How about a hot bath?"

"Too tired."

"Foot massage?"

Every chilled nerve in her body melted at the low hum of his voice. Even so, she knew when she had been bested by exhaustion. "All I want is a quick shower."

"Okay."

"And a full night's sleep with no one ringing the bell."

"That I can't promise."

"I know. I wish you could. I wish someone could make them leave me alone for just one day."

He pulled his head back and looked down at her, his rich brown eyes filled with passion and concern in equal measure. "That doesn't sound like you, Doc. Are you okay?"

"Yes, I'm fine—"

The incredulous look he gave her forbade any pretense. She didn't have the energy to pretend, anyway. "Very well. I am not fine. Far from it."

His hand glided from her waist to the small of her back as he casually ushered her to the divan. "No matter how tired you are, you won't sleep unless you talk it out."

"You know me too well."

His voice softened with his confident grin. "And yet I want to know you more."

While she sat where he directed, he plucked the footstool from her father's chair and set it in front of her. He patted it for her to prop up her feet and peeled off her stockings. "Tell me what happened."

She'd sworn to herself she would not complain, but the more he rubbed her sore feet, the more he watched her with those perfect eyes, the less resolve she had to resist. "I can't speak about my patients' details, of course, but today was full of the same rubbish as the past few weeks. This patient is nervous, that one is achy. No true malady. I'm not saving lives; I'm distributing common advice. It seems every appointment today ended with me telling the patient they are fine and the Land is fine and everything will be fine. Every appointment except one, that is."

He raised a black eyebrow. "Someone was seriously ill?"

"No, no. That patient was fine too. Very fine, indeed. I just meant that our appointment ended differently." She wasn't planning to say anything until breakfast tomorrow, so her father could hear the news at the same time as Connor, but the timing didn't seem to matter anymore. "I conducted Bethany's exam this afternoon, and she wanted me to tell you and Father the results."

He stopped rubbing her feet, his thumbs pausing at her insteps. "Is the baby okay?"

"Babies," she corrected. "I heard two heartbeats, felt two heads."

"Twins?"

She nodded. "Our Bethany will be twice blessed at once."

A spark of joy brightened his expression. "That's awesome! Everett must've been thrilled."

"Indeed, he was. Roseanne too. As were Bethany's friends, who devote an abundance of time to keeping her company. They won't let her lift a finger. Quite pampered, she is." She paused before her tone betrayed the jealousy igniting in her chest.

"Is it safe to announce?"

"There are definitely two babies. I leave it up to each mother whether she wants to announce the details, since no pregnancy is ever truly safe until the mother is delivered." She remembered her brother-in-law's jubilant response. "Before I left the Foster house for my next appointment, Everett had shouted the news to half of the farm hands working outside, so I'd say they are announcing the news to anyone who will listen."

"Good for him and Bethany!"

She'd spent the evening at three more house calls, trying to change her inward attitude while she worked, but the thick feeling inside her spirit wouldn't dissolve. "Yes, good for them."

Connor left her happy feet on the footstool and sat beside her. "Rejoice with those who rejoice, Doc, even when you've had a rough day."

"I know. I do." She leaned against his side. "I am happy for my sister and Everett. And for Mandy and Levi."

"Then what's wrong?"

How could she utter the words that she shouldn't be feeling?

She was supposed to be satisfied with the family God had given her, supposed to cherish her home, supposed to be content in the career she had chosen.

She wasn't supposed to feel this way. But when Connor stroked her aching shoulders, a reluctant response slipped from her tongue. "What bothers me... what has cast its shadow upon me is not that my dearest friend's nursery is expanding while mine is not; it isn't that two hearts beat in my sister's womb and she idles her afternoons in the company of friends while I work day and night; it is not that my young assistant glows with the thrill of discovery in the research my heart longs to do. It is that my life lacks the promise of possibility. I no longer awaken with the joy of wondering what newness might await me. I only work, work, work, and still the bell rings again."

Connor shifted to look into her eyes. "So, it's your life in general that upsets you?"

"No!" Her reflexive answer came with more volume than she intended. Her voice and posture obediently came under her control. "No, of course not."

Connor pressed his lips in a firm line and nodded, but disbelief glowed in his sidelong gaze.

That always irritated her. "You don't believe me? Fine. I'm just tired, that's all. I need sleep."

He shook his head. "You need rest."

"Same thing."

"No, it isn't."

When she let out an exhausted breath, he rubbed her back with his wide palm. That kept her from standing to leave the room. It always did.

The calm in his voice strengthened his words. "You've had way too many house calls since the haze arrived. People are anxious, and anxious people feel sickly. Since life is abnormal right now, it's time to change the way you work."

"How?"

"Instead of going to every person who calls for the doctor, insist they come to the medical office for treatment, unless it is a genuine emergency and they cannot travel."

"That wouldn't change the number of patients I see in a day."

"No, but it would cut out your travel time. Less time walking back and forth through the village or riding out to farms would give you more time at home or with your research or doing whatever you want to do."

"That sounds nice." She admired his logic and how easily he dissected her problems with her. Yet solutions were rarely as simple as he made them sound. "But I'm not sure it would be the right policy for my patients. It can be difficult for people to know if their loved one is experiencing a medical emergency. For example, most people in the village can't tell if someone is having a panic attack or a heart attack."

He nodded. "True, but what about appointments like the one you had with Bethany today? Couldn't she have come to the medical office? That would have saved you a mile ride out to the Foster farm."

"I don't want to make pregnant women walk in the cold."

"Everett has a wagon."

"It was snowing this afternoon."

"It's a covered wagon." He grinned and pointed a thumb over his shoulder. "She can ride in the back under a warm blanket. Her little gaggle of friends can ride back there with her and feed her grapes."

That got a chuckle out of her. "All right, fine. I see your point. I will think about it." A yawn interrupted her. "Tomorrow."

Connor stood and offered a hand to help her up. "It'll be okay. Try not to worry. Your workload will be lighter soon."

"I like your confidence." She followed him to the stairs with her eyes half closed. "I keep telling my anxious patients the haze won't be on the horizon forever."

"It won't. Mercer said the Global scientists believed the volcanic ash would dissipate within two years max."

She yawned again, then stopped at the stairs to look up at his caring face for one last boost of encouragement to end her day. "It has only been a few months; I might not have the endurance to continue this pace for another year or more."

A twinkle brightened his eyes. "You might not have to."

She gave his hand a squeeze. "Do you know something I don't?"

"Yes, but I can't give you details about my work, just like you can't tell me about your patients."

"Your work? Something from the elder meetings?" She used her last flicker of energy to try to get the secret out of him and trailed a finger along his angled jaw. "What is it?"

He kissed her forehead. "Don't worry about it tonight. Just take things one day at a time."

"I have no choice."

He brushed a stray strand of hair out of her face. "You really need a break soon. Do you have any appointments tomorrow?"

"Not yet."

"Take the day off." When she opened her mouth to protest, he raised a finger. "Unless there is an actual emergency, of course. But don't fill your day with office work. Let Sophia handle it. Just relax. Sleep in. Invite Mandy over for coffee like you used to. I'll take care of Andrew all day. No worries."

Her mouth had yet to close. A day without work? It was almost unthinkable these days.

And it was exactly what she would recommend for her patients, for him, for anyone else facing overwork. But for herself?

The fact that relaxing seemed impossible proved his point. She surrendered to his leadership. "Very well. But am I allowed to unbox our Christmas decorations?"

"Only if you find that relaxing."

"May I go to the library?"

"Only if you plan to read for pleasure."

The idea of not working for one day grew more appealing by the second. "All right, I will do as you say and take a day off work."

A grin flashed across his lips. "There's my girl." Before she could muster the energy to smile back, he scooped her into his arms and carried her upstairs.

CHAPTER THREE

All that came between Lydia and the ability to sleep past dawn was a keen sense of responsibility, an unpurgeable desire to beat the sunrise to her chores, and the bubbly laughter of her energetic son reverberating through the house. It was enough to fully awaken her mind.

She had to get up; she was taking a day of rest from her job, after all, not from life.

First light didn't illuminate the bedroom curtains like it used to before the haze, but her very marrow knew the hour. A deep breath confirmed it. The tantalizing aroma of Connor's famous fried eggs and sausage wafted up from the kitchen, drawing her head from beneath the pillow. She loved when her husband cooked breakfast. And when the bell remained silent all night.

Praise the Lord Almighty for glorious sleep!

She inched the covers away from her face for a full inhale and caught the bold undertone of her favorite morning beverage. Connor always brewed the coffee leaves twice as long as everyone in the Land. He said doing so recreated the strong taste of the ground coffee beans he was accustomed to brewing. It had taken him years to stop commenting on the strangeness of the Land's coffee leaf plant every time he brewed a pot, but lately he had settled into his life here—and the traditions here—more than she knew was possible.

And no longer did anyone doubt he would one day make an excellent overseer of Good Springs.

However, John Colburn was only in his fifties and in perfect health, so the day of Connor replacing him as village overseer was far in the future. For now, her adoring husband's leadership and wisdom were already a great asset to Good Springs. And to her. Including his instruction for her to pause her work for one day.

The warm mattress dipped as she sat on the edge of the bed and lowered her feet to the rag rug on the cold floor. Her toes begged to go back under the covers, but life drove her onward. Always, always onward.

Connor was right. She needed a day of rest.

As she dressed, she asked God to keep everyone in the village healthy today, not only for their sakes, but also for hers. Just one day without someone racing through the village to fetch her.

Scant morning light filtered through the window blinds in the parlor. The clock on the wall behind her father's empty chair claimed she had technically risen after the sun. The haze that loomed on the horizon made her doubt the clock's correctness.

She shuffled into the busy kitchen, the last member of the household to do so. Her father was standing near his seat at the head of the table, pouring steaming coffee into waiting cups. Little Andrew was kneeling in his chair, hunkered over a ready plate, his bottom bouncing, unable to hold himself still.

Sophia was spreading an array of jam jars around the bread basket at the center of the long dining table. "Good morning, Doctor Bradshaw," her assistant greeted her before the men noticed her entry.

Connor turned from the stove, where a pan of sausage sizzled to perfection. A grin touched his lips the instant their eyes met. With a quick wiggle of his brow, he reminded her of last night, then he glanced at his culinary creation. "I hope you're hungry."

She met him by the hot stove for a quick kiss. "You made enough food for the entire squadron."

He winked like he did whenever she hinted at his former life. "You know it, babe."

Andrew hopped out of his chair and ran to them with his plate. "Fill mine full, Daddy."

Lydia lifted the ceramic dish from his little hands, praying a spill or breakage didn't steal her precious morning time. As soon as the plate was safely on the countertop, she captured him for a hug, but he was too spirited to tolerate a cuddle from his mother. When he slipped from her embrace and dashed back to the table, she looked up at Connor. "I miss when he was a baby and could be held all day."

He shrugged. "I don't. He's finally getting big enough to do cool stuff."

"Cool stuff?"

"Yeah. While you enjoy the day to yourself, I'm taking him horseback riding." He casually piled the contents of the pan onto a serving dish. "He's strong enough to grip the reins."

Her hand reflexively covered her stomach. Connor eyed her, so she halted her nervous gesture and straightened her posture. "Hold on to him, please. I don't want any trauma patients today, and especially not my only child."

Connor responded with a half-incredulous, half-confident look that put her worries in their place and her heart in his hands. "I won't let him get hurt."

After John said the blessing, Connor filled Lydia's plate with more food than she usually ate even at dinnertime. She savored every bite. Andrew emptied his plate too, though half of its contents were scattered on the floor around his chair.

When Lydia stood to clean the mess, Connor stopped her. "Freeze right there! I'm on kid duty today. Remember?"

"No, you said I could do whatever I enjoy today, and what I most enjoy is taking care of my family."

That brought a quick smile to Connor's face. "Nice try, Doc." Before she could protest, he had his napkin to the floor. "I'll handle this mess."

"What about the barn chores?"

"I'll handle those too."

She nodded her resignation and carried the dirty dishes to the sink.

Sophia intercepted her before she could rinse the first plate. "And I will take care of all the house chores today."

"We both will," John said as he left his seat at the table. "While Sophia cleans the kitchen, I will dust the parlor. You should go to the library and enjoy a quiet hour before anyone else is there—just like you used to."

A quiet hour in the library sounded lovely, and it was exactly what she had hoped for. She held up surrendering hands. "It seems you all are in on Connor's kind plan. I would be foolish to resist."

Andrew had already forgotten about breakfast and was pretending to fly his wooden toy airplane around the room. As he whooshed past Lydia, she kissed him. "How about you, young man? Will you let me have a day of rest?"

He giggled and sprung away from her while flying the toy high over his head. "Go sleep now, Mama!"

She chuckled. "I'm not sleeping today. I'm resting."

He ran into the parlor before she could say another word. Her little boy was definitely his father's son. Perhaps, if they ever had a second child, God might give her a little girl, a daughter who would stay cuddly and gentle through childhood, and then one day, maybe, she would want to follow in her mother's footsteps.

Smudged gray light brightened into crisp morning beams as the sun rose above the haze to conquer the Land's bane for the next few hours. The clear sky overhead breathed a soft warmth upon Good Springs, melting the dusting of snow that dotted the grass along the road. Perhaps a day of sunshine would restore the villagers' spirits, feed the earth's vegetation, and give Lydia some spark of hope that life in the Land would return to normal.

She needed to feel hope—a hope that couldn't be smothered when the afternoon sunshine was once again swallowed by the haze that waited on the western horizon. The hope she needed to feel was the sort only God could give.

Might He?

Oh, how she'd begged!

Her heavy woolen shawl felt unnecessary with the fine sunlight surrounding her while she strolled from the Colburn property to her favorite place in the village. She shifted her satchel strap on her shoulder so she could loosen the shawl and let it hang open over her day dress.

Sandy gravel crunched beneath her boots and soon gave way to cobblestones as she walked through the center of the village. The chapel's white steeple rose into the air like a beacon for all who needed solace. The historic house of worship held a lifetime of sweet memories, but her soul's consolation usually came inside another of the village's old buildings.

Though a humble structure, the stone library was her most beloved refuge, more like a friend than a building. It sheltered the few precious books the Founders brought with them when they sailed from America and the many journals written over the seven generations since then. It had also sheltered her lonely heart during her years of study while apprenticing to become a doctor.

The tapered door to the library was narrow and made of thick planks salvaged from the *Providence*, the ship that carried the Founders to these shores. Sometimes the door stuck, especially when damp weather swelled the wood. To her, the effort it took to open the ancient door was proof a person had to want to go inside. Knowledge rarely came without effort.

She turned the squeaky doorknob and pushed her way into the stale and stately room. The shuttered windows blocked any sunlight from reaching the crowded bookcases. Normally, the pressman would have lit the hanging lanterns by this hour and would be working at his press in the back room, but he had traveled up north to visit kin for the month of December. Wise choice. Perhaps it was warmer up there.

Lydia didn't need to leave town to find peace; she only needed an hour alone in this blessed book vault. She flopped her decades-old leather satchel onto the center of the study table and ignited one oil lamp and then another. Two provided enough light for her to peruse the rows of time-tested books smiling at her from the shelves.

Her fingers skimmed the spines of the medical books and journals from the many physicians who had come before her. Someday, her journals would join them and await the curious fingertips of future generations to pluck them from the rows.

She halted at a title that caught her attention. *Observations in Fertility by Doctor Abraham Ashton.*

She slipped the hundred-year-old book from the shelf and sat on one of the wooden stools at the study table, tucking her skirt around her legs. The book's advice on fertility concerns was much of the same as others written during that time, claiming a close correlation between anger and infertility and stating that mentally taxing work stole a woman's maternal energy and prevented pregnancy.

She wasn't an angry person, and her mind was accustomed to taxing work—craved it even.

Connor always said those types of claims had been disproven by modern science, and there was nothing wrong with their fertility.

Perhaps he was right. He usually was.

She clapped the book shut and returned it to its place. After a quick scan of the other medical titles, she stepped back to take in the entire section. Six shelves from floor to ceiling filled with the scientific observations of many generations, and none of it called to her.

So maybe it wasn't the inability to expand her family that was at the root of her discontent. She wandered to the window that faced the school and unlatched the shutters.

The village's young scholars arrived for their last day of learning before their scheduled summer break. Though there might not be a proper summer this year, many of the children would still spend the time working alongside their parents on their farms or in their workshops.

The Cotter children walked like a row of ducklings following their mother. The young Miss Grace waved to a girl ahead and rushed to greet her. Seeing Grace relaxed and happy, chatting with a friend warmed Lydia's heart. Even if her work was less exciting and seemingly unending of late, she was still making a difference.

Maybe her work wasn't the source of her malaise, either.

She ambled to the next bookcase and perused its rows and rows of ladies' journals. The older the spine, the quicker her fingers were to pull it from the shelf. Most of the recipes and housekeeping tips were common knowledge now, but a book of Christmas traditions from the Founders caught her eye.

She sat at the study table again and turned the pages without reading much. She didn't need to learn new traditions, only to honor those from her mother and grandmothers. There was a chest of Christmas decorations in the attic at home, and her father and Connor had enjoyed the feast she'd prepared the last two years, using handed-down recipes.

After returning the ladies' journals to the shelf, she closed the window shutters and sat at the study table under the light of the oil lamps, empty handed. The desire to learn something new had always driven her here, but it wasn't something new that would regenerate her spirit. She already had all she needed in life: a loving husband, a child, meaningful work.

Perhaps simply being at home would satisfy her soul.

Closing her satchel, she stood and slid the wooden stool under the study table. Her fingers traced the wood grain along the table's edge. The quiet of the library had settled her thoughts, and now all she wanted was to carry that quiet home with her.

The house was empty when she returned, save for the lingering aroma of breakfast. The men were probably in the paddock with the horses, and Sophia would be in the medical cottage. The kitchen was clean and the parlor dusted, just as they had promised.

The sunlight filling the house all morning fueled Lydia's homemaking. She had started the laundry and spread an abundant luncheon on the buffet when everyone returned to the kitchen at noon. After lunch, she would have plenty of time to unbox those Christmas decorations and honor the memory of her mother.

While Connor washed Andrew's hands at the sink and John carried in a pitcher of milk from the cellar, Sophia whirled through the kitchen door, cheeks blushing and smile gleaming.

All eyes landed on her, but she only looked at Lydia. "Oh, Doctor Bradshaw! It's finally happened. I'm so happy!" Her smile disappeared as if a thought had shocked her. "And I'm so sorry too."

CHAPTER FOUR

Lydia's breath lodged between a laugh to share Sophia's bubbly joy and a cry for the sudden sorrow behind her eyes. She exhaled softly in her best bedside manner and gave her young assistant's shaky hand a gentle squeeze. "There now, Sophia. What could possibly make you so happy and so sad at the same time?"

Sophia's glowing smile returned. "We're getting married—Nicholas and I! This Sunday after the church service," she looked at John, who had paused in the doorway, "if you will perform the ceremony."

John's trimmed gray beard rounded with his kind grin. "I will."

Sophia snapped her gaze back to Lydia. "And if you approve, of course."

Lydia's insides flopped with a tide of quick emotions. She struggled to keep her voice level. "Surely, you don't need my approval to get married."

Sophia twined her fingers around and around themselves like an eager child begging a parent for a puppy. "I know this is all so sudden. Nicholas and I had agreed we wouldn't speak of marriage until he finished restoring the house and preparing his land for a flock," she glanced between Lydia and John and Connor as her chatter picked up speed, "but then when the haze came, he worked longer hours to keep himself occupied, so it's ready much sooner than we thought it would be."

Lydia stacked plates on the buffet and straightened the silverware to keep her hands busy. "Don't you want to observe the tradition of having a preparation week? That way, the village can make sure you have everything you need to begin your life together."

Sophia shrugged. "We have all we need. Nicholas has been preparing for this since he inherited the cabin."

"What about your relatives? Won't they need time to travel to Good Springs?"

She shook her head and the chestnut bun atop her head wobbled. "None of our relatives will come here for the wedding. Nicholas's parents say they are too busy with their farm in Woodland, and my parents... well, you know." She snatched a tea towel from a hook by the sink and dried Andrew's clean hands. "It doesn't matter to us though, because we think of you all as our family. And the Fosters too, of course. Truly, we are most eager to start a family of our own."

Andrew giggled as Sophia made silly faces at him.

Lydia's stomach soured while she watched her son enjoy the attention of her soon-to-be former assistant. She would no longer have Sophia around to stay in the cottage with overnight patients nor to babysit Andrew when patients needed house calls. The entire reason Lydia could provide the amount of care for the village that she did was because she had Sophia's reliable help. And now she was losing it.

She looked to Connor, hoping he might say something to Sophia about leaving so abruptly. He only dried his hands and smiled at Sophia. "Congrats, Soph! That's awesome. I had a talk with Nicholas awhile back—*the* talk—and told him you're like a little sister to me. He caught my drift."

Sophia's blush shone. "Oh, I have no doubts about Nicholas's faithfulness. But thank you. Thank you all for everything. And Dr. Bradshaw, I am sorry for my sudden departure." She turned to John without waiting for Lydia to reply. "Nicholas asked if we might borrow your wagon on Saturday to move my things to his house—to our house." She giggled. "Oh, how lovely that is to say—our house!"

John agreed to lend the wagon and added his congratulations. Connor was all smiles for Sophia, and Andrew was all giggles, though he wouldn't understand why they were so happy. Lydia could understand, but she couldn't hold her peace any longer. "Why the rush to leave us?"

Sophia kept chatting while she exuberantly hoisted Andrew to her hip and showed him the food Lydia had spread on the buffet. "Everett can only give Nicholas a few days' leave because of the shearing. That's why we need to borrow the wagon on Saturday, especially to move my grandfather's desk."

It wasn't the answer Lydia was looking for. "But why *this* Saturday?"

Sophia wrinkled her nose at Andrew, barely paying attention to the conversation. "I will want my desk in my new home."

"On your wedding night?"

Connor flashed Lydia a quick frown—the one that warned her when her emotions were clouding her logic.

She tamed her tone of voice, but couldn't tamp down what was bubbling up inside. "Of course, you should take your things to your new home. But I thought you and

Nicholas agreed you would still assist me in the medical office for a few hours a week after you are married, at least until you find yourself in the family way."

Sophia's sweet smile clung to her teeth. "Well, he has earned his own flock and will leave the Fosters' employ as soon as the new shepherds are trained. Then, I will help him with our farm work. I get to plant my own vegetable garden. With all that Bailey taught me, I should be able to grow enough produce for us, even during this haze."

John raised both palms, halting Lydia's unasked questions and Sophia's play with Andrew. He said the blessing, then helped Andrew with his lunch plate at the buffet. After Lydia filled their cups, she picked at her scant lunch, her stomach still full from her feast at breakfast.

While Sophia prattled on to John about her, and Nicholas's life plans, Connor leaned close to Lydia. "Don't worry about the future. Just be happy for them. Besides, I received some good news this morning."

It may have been the nearness of his whisper or the hope in his tone or both, but her spirit instantly lifted. "What is your good news?"

He sent a forkful of potato salad into his mouth and shook his head, a secret grin cocking one corner of his lips.

She loved that grin. "Tell me now."

"Nope, no business today. It's your day off work, remember?"

Whatever it was, the news had a sparkle in his eye that lured her to beg. "Have you heard something over the radio about the haze leaving? If so, please tell me now. I could really use some good news." When Sophia paused her chatter, Lydia forced a smile. "Not that your news isn't wonderful. It is. I'm thrilled for you and Nicholas. You both deserve much happiness."

"Amen!" Connor lifted his water cup and affected his voice with great pomp. "To a happy marriage!"

Sophia smiled graciously at Connor's demonstrative toast and lifted her cup. "Amen!"

Andrew lifted his little cup and used the same tone as his daddy. "Amen more milk!"

While they all laughed at Andrew's cuteness, Lydia sent Connor her own furtive smile. "Please, tell me."

He shook his head once. "The bell didn't ring all night and no one went to your office all morning. Just enjoy chilling out at long as you can. Today is about you resting."

"And that makes it the perfect time to get good news. Let's hear it. Please."

Connor flicked a glance at Sophia and John, who had returned to their own conversation. Then he sighed. "Can you at least wait until after lunch?"

His plate was almost empty, and she wasn't hungry. Lunch was over, as far as she was concerned. "I'm done."

"I want to tell you in private."

She pointed her chin at the kitchen door. "My office?"

"If you insist."

"I do."

"Okay, okay." He swallowed the last of his lunch, stood from the table, and took her hand. "We'll be right back," he announced to the others.

Andrew scurried down from his chair. "Take me too, Daddy."

John caught him by his shirt tail. "No, you stay here with me."

Connor pointed his son back to his chair. "If you finish your food, Grandpa will let you have dessert."

While her husband and father corralled her son, Lydia's gaze fixed on Sophia. There was nothing so distasteful as disappointment, whether in the heart or in the air. She shouldn't be upset that the girl was getting married. She had known this was coming. A more generous notice would have been professional, but she had hired Sophia straight out of school; any professionalism was from her own teaching.

In the few steps from the kitchen door to her medical office, Lydia's heart softened. Her situation wasn't Sophia's fault. Lydia had allowed herself to get too accustomed to having an assistant. She had worked for several years without help in the office and could do it again. She had her husband and her father to watch Andrew, and apparently God had limited their family to one child for His purpose, and she must accept that too.

Yes, her work would go on just as it used to. As long as she was able, she would be the physician of Good Springs, with all the overwhelming responsibility and hard-won respect that position afforded. Her village needed her; not just any doctor—her. She would never bemoan that privilege again.

Connor opened the medical cottage door for her, and she stepped into her office. The minty aroma of gray leaf medicine greeted her like an old friend. Though she'd only been away from her office for one morning, it felt good to be back.

She sat at her desk out of habit, then instantly stood, remembering their reason for coming out here. "So, what is this news? Is the haze lifting? Did the Land's overseers confirm you as Father's successor?"

He opened his hand to her desk chair. "Have a seat." A commanding tone edged his voice, making him sound more like he did when he talked with his security team than with her.

She sat as he'd directed. "I thought you said you received good news today."

"It was good news, but you have to trust me while I explain, okay?"

Her heart pounded hard, remembering every moment of thrill and terror they had been through since he arrived from the outside world over five years ago. "I do trust you."

He lowered himself to the chair beside her desk and crossed his legs, ankle over knee. "When you were pregnant with Andrew, some on the elder council questioned your ability to be a mother and Good Springs's only physician. Late in your pregnancy, you couldn't have ridden out to patients if there had been an emergency."

When she started to defend herself, he raised a palm and kept talking. "It all worked out fine, I know. Your dad and I both stood up for you in the council meetings the entire time. And Sophia came on as your assistant soon after Andrew was born, which has been great. In the meantime though, a few of the elders took the matter to the Lands' other overseers. They said a married female doctor was simply a mother with too many obligations."

"How dare they!"

"Your dad and I know what you're capable of, so we told them you could do the job just fine. We didn't think it would be necessary to bring in a second physician."

"Good."

"But once the haze set in and the harsh winter came, more people had medical complaints than ever, and your time has been stretched thin." He propped his elbows on his knees and leaned forward, his eyes dark with earnestness. "Lydia, your dad and I can see the stress you're under."

Her lungs burned with the scream she held in. She was a professional and had to behave as such, especially while that very ability was being questioned. Her toes curled inside her shoes. "The Land might be under unusual circumstances at present, but I am quite able to manage."

Neither his posture nor his gaze changed. "You shouldn't have to do the job of two people. And with Sophia leaving, you'll have even more work."

Frustration seeped into her voice. "I cannot see how you and Father joining with the village elders in believing I'm unfit for my job is good news."

He leaned away. "We do not believe you are unfit— just overwhelmed. So, for your sake, we agreed to take recommendations for medical apprentices from other Land physicians."

She shot out of her chair. "Without my input?"

He patted the air like her father always did. "You need another doctor to divide the work with, especially when there are difficult surgeries to perform or multiple patients to handle. Plus, this will give you more time for other things in life—like you were talking about last night."

"This better not be your good news."

He withdrew a folded letter from his back pocket. "Revel delivered the mail this morning. The Stonehill doctor's son has been fully trained for years, and they also have an apprentice who is coming to the end of his training. He still needs to be titled. All the Land's overseers have agreed this apprentice should complete his training under you to gain the village's trust and then be titled by you in Good Springs."

The optimism in his voice made her teeth grind. She paced to the window to look at something other than his face. "When we were courting, you encouraged me to focus on my work. You recognized that I'm passionate about medicine and saving people. You said that life is pitifully mediocre without passion and that I should let no one take that away from me. You said you wouldn't take my passion away from me or take me away from my village. How could you go behind my back like this now and ruin my career?"

She didn't hear him leave his chair, but his next words came from inches behind her. "This won't ruin your career; it will save it. It was either we choose a second physician to complement your work or they would select your replacement. The good news is: your father and I found the person we think you will like best."

Her temples throbbed as tears welled in her eyes. No matter how hard she tried to stop herself from crying, her face betrayed her. "When is he coming? This new doctor to take my place?"

He smoothed her tense shoulders with his warm hands. "No one is taking your place. Not anytime soon. But someday you will need a replacement. You know the Land's tradition requires you, requires everyone to pass on their trade, and you—"

"If only I could have selected my own apprentice here, but there isn't a single student interested in apprenticing in medicine, and Andrew is not yet three. Besides, he will probably train to succeed you, not me." Once again, her anger at someone else turned on herself. "I know the tradition, and no, I wasn't following it. I guess I thought since I received my title five years ago, it was too soon for me to train my own apprentice. But now I've missed my chance."

He turned her reluctant body, keeping his palms firmly on her shoulders. "No, you haven't missed your chance. As soon as this guy is titled, you can train another apprentice. You can train a brood of aspiring doctors and have them following you from house call to house call. But for now, you must accept the new physician when he gets here and put him to good use." He gazed at her, his compassion and authority unwavering. "Because if you work yourself sick, you'll be of no use to anyone."

She opened her mouth to tell him she didn't like being forced into this and that it was done behind her back and that she felt betrayed because he and her father had known about it all along and kept her in the dark, but a knock on the office door silenced her complaints. "Come in."

Mark Cotter stepped inside but kept one hand on the doorknob. "Pardon, Dr. Bradshaw, but it's Mr. Vestal. It was my day to help with some of the work around his orchard. I went into the house to check on him when we were done. He's barely able to carry on a conversation, wouldn't lift his head off the pillow. He didn't want me to send for you, says he's just tired. We all knew that's not true. I had one of the men stay with him, seeing as how his kin haven't arrived yet."

Lydia left Connor by the window and checked her medical bag, which waited on the worktable. "Thank you, Mark. I'll go to him directly."

Mark thanked her, nodded his acknowledgment to Connor, and left as swiftly as he'd come.

Connor stepped to the open door. "I'll tack up Dapple for you."

"Thank you."

"Sorry you didn't get an entire day off."

"I'm not. It won't be long before people rush to the new doctor for help. I may as well enjoy my position while I still have it."

CHAPTER FIVE

The new iron cookstove in the corner of Philip's two-room parsonage had an oven large enough for only one pan and a stovetop wide enough for only two pots. To Philip, the humble stove was more than the overseer of the Land's smallest village could ask for. The kind people of Stonehill who had donated the stove to the Falls Creek parsonage surely knew Philip had not yet been blessed with a wife to make the most of such a fine cooker. As a bachelor, he either dined at the inn or made sandwiches from leftovers from the cellar's icebox.

So far, he'd only used the cookstove to boil water for his morning coffee. The generous donors must have shared his hope that he would someday—someday soon, Lord willing—know the joy of marriage and family.

While he dusted the much appreciated stove, he imagined his future wife whipping up a scrumptious breakfast of baked oatmeal, boiled eggs, and fried potatoes while their children set the table.

His dust rag stilled as he pictured the scene.

They'd have two girls and a boy. He glanced from the front room to the bedroom. The house would need an addition if his dream of having a family came true.

After dusting the sparsely furnished house and sweeping the floors, he shook the broom outside and scanned the hazy mid-morning horizon. Above the grayish smudge that circled the earth, the sun glistened from the crisp circle above. God had allowed them a miracle with that window to the heavens during this tragic time on earth. Philip prayed for the people of the Land as they planted seed not knowing if it would yield a crop, and for the people not in the Land who, according to Bailey's report of the outside world, were drenched in the darkness of a volcanic winter.

Across the road the inn's noble shadow stretched almost to the stable block, and the stable's shadow blanketed the paddock to its west. The stable's high arched door had been rolled open, but the horses hadn't been put out to the pasture yet.

Philip stepped back inside the parsonage and checked the mantel clock. Already ten. Solo must not have any help in the stables today.

Without another thought of his house chores, Philip tugged on his old boots, slapped on his round-brimmed hat, and traipsed across the road, buttoning his work coat as he went. The sun's warmth gave his fingers pause before he fastened the coat's top button. Perhaps this near-summer day might warm up after all. Oh, how he had prayed for one fine day!

The pungent mixture of old hay and fresh manure greeted him potently. He stepped into the stables high open entry, which made him feel childishly short. It was a long-fought feeling he'd often surrendered to the Lord, who kindly reminded him that what he lacked in stature, he made up for in strength. And in faith, when strength faltered.

He sidestepped an empty feed bucket. "Solomon?"

"Back here."

Philip passed the front row of horse stalls and turned right to follow the stable manager's voice. A bay gelding snorted at him as he passed. He didn't recognize the horse, nor the next one. They probably belonged to the Vestal siblings, who were staying the week at the inn.

Sunlight flushed through the open door at the long end of the stable's L-shaped block. It highlighted a row of stalls.

Philip found Solo in the second to last stall and stopped at the gate. "No traders stayed to work today?"

Solo shoveled straw and manure from the floor into a waiting wheelbarrow. "Nope. The only guests are the three folks heading to Good Springs the day after Christmas. Noah is helping Isaac in the barn, and his sisters are in the laundry house. Caroline and Lena, I think their names are."

"Lena," Philip whispered with a half-held breath. Finally, a name to put with the petite woman's mysterious yet familiar eyes. Why she had captured his attention, he did not know. Feeling Solo's quick gaze, he halted his reverie at once and lifted a spare shovel that was propped against the opposite stall. "Which stalls still need to be cleaned out?"

"Most of them. I can take care of it easy enough if you'll fetch a load of fresh hay and then take the horses to the pasture."

Philip returned the shovel to the wall and pointed at the door that led out to the barn. "A load of hay. Of course. Oats too?"

"Nah, just the hay. Cart's outside."

While Philip strode to the door, Solo started whistling a Christmas song. The melody faded behind Philip as he crossed the threshold into the sunshine. Though the warmth felt divine against his face, his feet never tarried when there was stable work to do. Of all the chores around the inn and of all the people to work with, he most enjoyed spreading hay in the stables with Solo.

He grabbed the long cart by its splintery handle and dragged it into the barn. As his eyes adjusted to the lack of light in the barn, he tugged on his work gloves. "Isaac?"

An unfamiliar voice came from the milking pens. "Isaac went to the west field."

Philip followed the voice and found Noah filling feeder bins for an eager milk cow.

"Ah, Mr. Vestal. How do you do this morning?"

"I do all right." He flashed an amused grin, his teeth unnaturally straight. "And my father is Mr. Vestal. Call me Noah."

"If you wish." Philip tapped the cart's handle. "Solo sent me for a load of hay."

Noah lifted his chin at a haystack against the far wall. "I just brought that down from the loft. Help yourself."

"Excellent. Thank you." Philip turned to walk away, then stopped. Something unique about Noah's voice reminded him of someone. He tried to think. Yes, that was it. He drew out some words a bit like Connor Bradshaw. Perhaps they had spent time together and Noah had taken on his way of talking. Philip looked back at him. "Where did you say you're from?"

"Northcrest."

"On your way to Good Springs?"

"That's right."

"Are you acquainted with Connor Bradshaw? The outsider who lives there?"

"No."

"Why, Mr. Bradshaw and our Bailey are the only people I've ever met from the outside world. Surely, you have heard of him."

Noah spread the hay into the feeders with quick movements to avoid the pushy cow beside him. "Heard of him. Not acquainted."

"I'm sure you will get to know him very well once you are in Good Springs. He is training under John Colburn to one day be the village overseer."

Noah made no reply.

Often, traders and travelers kept silent as they worked. Philip understood.

Still, something about Noah, something he hadn't noticed before, seemed familiar. Maybe not quite familiar. He felt like he was about to remember something, or forget something—that foggy flash of memory one can't grasp long enough to decipher if it is from life or a dream or a story told so well it left the impression of reality.

Not wanting to seem as odd as he felt, Philip broke his gaze and dragged the cart away, trying all the while to think of what struck him about the Vestals. Perhaps it was the eyes. Noah had the same hazel eyes as his younger sister, Lena. But that wasn't what piqued his curiosity today. It was something in the voice this time, not in tone but in rhythm.

That was why Philip had thought of Connor Bradshaw, but since Noah said he had no connection, it was wrong.

The empty cart rattled on the barn's dirt floor as Philip pulled it to the haystack. Once full and heavy, it rumbled as he pushed it back to the door. Before leaving, he looked back for Noah, but the hungry cow was alone in the milking pen and the gate was closed.

Philip's leg muscles warmed as he shoved the long cart from the barn to the stable block's side door. Intending only to glance, he looked toward the laundry house across the yard. Solo had said the Vestal sisters were working there today. Wide rectangles of crisp linen flapped on the clotheslines outside the laundry house. Between the swaying sheets, he caught a glimpse of the two ladies working. Only Caroline looked up from her laundry. She smiled at him and gave a quick wave as if they were old friends.

He tapped his hat brim in response and rolled the cart into the stable block.

Something about the Vestal siblings held his curiosity. They might simply be a family moving from one village to another, but for some reason he wanted to know more. Perhaps the Lord had put them on his heart because they needed his counsel or prayer. Or perhaps he needed them somehow, but for what he could not imagine.

Whatever it was, his curiosity was only growing. If the youngest sister was shy and the older brother disinclined to speak, perhaps it was the middle sibling, the outgoing Caroline, who might answer his questions.

* * *

The sun shone brightly for the second day in a row, warming the air but unable to penetrate the frost that was thickening over Lydia's life. Though spending last night in the armchair next to the elderly Mr. Vestal's deathbed had proved sleepless, it had given her time away from home and the traitors therein. But now back in her office, the answers were no clearer.

How could her father erase her career and her husband not only go along with the scheme, but also think it a fine idea?

She shoved away from her desk and smoothed the flyaway tresses that escaped her exhausted chignon. Using the reflective glass door of the medical supply cabinet over her worktable, she repositioned the wearied hairpins. Her puffy eyes looked just as tired and begged her not to let resentment fester.

She held her own gaze in the reflection. No, Connor was not a traitor, nor was her father. They had done what they thought was best for the village. She knew that. They knew she knew that. Still, it didn't take the sting out of having the purpose bled out of her life's work, and all without her knowledge or consent.

A figure moved past the window, then the office door opened. Sophia was back from her sister's house already.

Lydia smoothed her bodice and swallowed her discontent. "You're back sooner than expected. Did it go well?"

"Alice was in one of her moods, and the children were having their afternoon nap. So, I simply accepted the wedding dress, thanked her, and said I would try it on here." She switched a tissue-wrapped parcel to the other arm as she closed the office door behind her. "Alice is almost as fine a seamstress as Grandmother was, so I'm sure it will fit perfectly."

Though Sophia's young lips had rarely stopped smiling since her engagement to Nicholas, the sadness of having no loving relatives with whom to share her happy occasion must have weighed down her heart. Lydia enjoyed her friendships with all of her siblings and couldn't imagine living far from her father. Her mother hadn't been at her wedding because she was in Heaven. Sophia's mother wouldn't be at her wedding because she was absorbed in a disgraceful lifestyle.

Again, Lydia's heart softened to the young woman's situation. While Sophia removed her shawl, Lydia held the dress for her. "I'm sure it is beautiful. You will be a splendid bride. Go upstairs and try it on. If you need any alterations, I'm happy to help you."

Sophia beamed. "You would? Oh, how kind! Thank you, Dr. Bradshaw."

Within minutes she returned from her room upstairs, wearing a simple but stunning creamy white dress edged with delicate yellow lace. "Do you think Nicholas will like it?"

"Like it? He won't be able to take his eyes off you." Lydia's fingers immediately checked the seams and assessed the fit. "Alice did an excellent job."

Sophia fluffed the skirts and turned quickly to make the hem swirl. "I saw two weddings last year, and both brides wore blue lace, but I wanted yellow to match the flowers Nicholas gave me the first time he showed me his house, I mean, our house."

Lydia wagged a finger. "Well, it isn't your house yet. Soon. Very soon, but not yet."

"Yes, only two more days to Sunday. Can you believe it? I'll be married!"

"No, I can't." The resentment threatened to resurface, so she returned to her desk to gather her wits. She was a professional. Dr. Ashton had trained her well, especially on how to remain self-controlled in difficult circumstances. She casually flipped through her calendar, reminding herself of her work. "So many women in the village are with child at present. We are expecting several births in the next few weeks. Each of these ladies will want me there for the delivery and you there assisting me, not some man they don't know. Won't you please consider staying on for a few weeks after the wedding?"

Sophia continued fanning her wedding dress and watching the silky fabric drape. "Nicholas is quite sure we should begin our life together as we intend to go on. I will want to please my husband."

What could she say when everything she'd been taught conflicted with everything she wanted? "Yes, of course. And so you should. Nicholas will want to please you too. He has always been aware of the importance of our work, and of how much you needed and valued your position. Perhaps, given the present circumstances of the Land, he would be willing to postpone the wedding until after you've fulfilled your duties here."

"I haven't fulfilled my duties?"

Lydia stood to be eye-to-eye with Sophia, but kept her tone friendly as not to put her on the defensive. "Your daily duties, yes. But in long-term cases, such as pregnancy, the patients prefer for their care to go unchanged. I wouldn't want the presence of a new physician to be upsetting to a laboring mother. Would you?"

Sophia stopped playing with her wedding dress. "No, I suppose not. But Nicholas says he heard that the elder council approved bringing another physician to Good Springs long before we set our date to wed."

Lydia plopped back into her seat. "Did everyone know but me?"

Sophia knelt swiftly. "Oh, no, Dr. Bradshaw. He only heard about the new physician this week after Connor told you and then you told me." She rubbed Lydia's arm as if consoling a child instead of a superior. "I wish I could do something to help you. I'd make this new fellow turn around on the road and go home before he arrived in Good Springs if I could. But I can't. Even if I stayed on for a year, the elders wouldn't change their plan because I'm not a physician. Not even close. I'm so sorry. Truly."

"It's not your fault, Sophia. The elders wanted Good Springs to have another doctor when I was carrying Andrew." She patted Sophia's hand and straightened up in her chair. "The council can bring in a trained apprentice for me to polish and title, if that is what they wish. But I have worked hard to earn the village's respect as the Land's first female doctor. I have no intention of letting the people down or of letting my position go."

Sophia stood and crossed her arms in solidarity. "And so you shouldn't!"

Suddenly energized, Lydia stood too. "At last, an ally!"

"Of course, I am your ally. You taught me all I know. I'll always be on your side."

"What's to be done, then?" Lydia asked aloud, though she doubted Sophia could contribute any ideas of worth. "The new man is on his way and will take my place— perhaps not immediately, but eventually."

Sophia tapped a finger on her chin as she wandered to the worktable. "It is your having too much work that is the council's reason for bringing in a second physician, correct?"

"Yes and," she hated to admit it to herself, let alone to her assistant, "and that's also the reason I've been out of sorts lately."

Sophia pointed to a stack of patient charts. "As I studied all the files you had me read, I discovered a pattern to the complaints—"

"Anxiety in the young, depression in the aged."

"Precisely."

As awkward as it felt to let Sophia walk her through a problem, she had to see where this was headed. If nothing else came of it, at least Sophia would know her loyalty was appreciated. She mirrored Sophia's thoughtful pose. "Doubtless, this is all due to the haze."

Sophia nodded with growing confidence. "Indeed. And in all our research with the gray leaf medicine, we theorized that the amount of scent molecules released naturally during the tree's growth cycle was enough to have a calming effect on those nearby."

Lydia's insides jolted. She reached for a vial of the sparkling gaseous vapor they had collected weeks ago. "Since the haze has shortened our daylight hours, the gray leaf trees might have gone dormant."

"Which means—"

"Which means the villagers were neurologically accustomed to high levels of gray leaf molecules in the air after living near the gray leaf forest all their lives. If those levels have dropped, it might be affecting everyone's mood."

"Exactly!"

Her heart thudded as she pulled Sophia into a quick hug. "You brilliant girl!"

"Oh, my! I don't know about brilliant, but—"

Any trace of betrayal and—dare she admit it?—bitterness evaporated from Lydia's spirit. She grabbed her silver pen from its holder and made notes as quickly as thoughts flooded her mind. This was not only the cure for the villagers' ailments and her workload, but also the new discovery she needed to spark her verve. "We can't stimulate the entire forest into its growth cycle without the amount of natural light required, but we can force seedlings in the greenhouse like Bailey showed us. If we can get a sapling in the windowsill of every room in every village house, perhaps it will add enough of the gray leaf molecules to indoor air to provide the relief people need."

"Bailey already has a greenhouse full of gray leaf saplings out at Falls Creek since the terribly cold winter halted their planting project. Maybe she could have them sent here."

"Excellent idea! I'll send a message to Falls Creek with Revel when he leaves in the morning." She scooped up her notebook and headed for the door. "In the meantime, we must start as many new plants in the greenhouse as we can."

Sophia clasped her hands together. "Oh, no! Dr. Bradshaw, wait!"

"What is it?"

The color drained from Sophia's rosy cheeks, along with her glee. "If the level of gray leaf molecules in the air has decreased enough to affect us physically, and if those molecules are part of what keeps the Land hidden, does that mean—"

"That the Land could be discovered by the outside world?" Lydia leaned against the door as the thought sucked the joy out of her lungs. "It might. Go to the greenhouse to see what supplies we need to force the saplings. I'll be back before my next appointment, but I must speak with Connor at once."

CHAPTER SIX

The parlor was quiet when Lydia entered, save for soft snoring coming from her father's armchair. John was asleep with his head against the back of the chair, and Andrew was asleep on the rug beside his grandfather's footstool. Stacks of wooden blocks dotted the parlor floor as if a mighty playtime war had been waged, the fortresses laid bare, and the townsfolk plundered.

Such would be Lydia's career if she couldn't help her community. Worse yet, such would be the Land if it became visible to the outside world.

Her father and son both looked too content dozing to be awakened. Connor would be at the chapel. He would have the best hypothesis regarding the gray leaf molecules and the atmospheric anomaly that hid the Land. She could think of nothing else, plan nothing else until she knew if their very lives were in jeopardy.

She left a note on the kitchen table for John and marched to the chapel, clutching her notebook as if it contained a treasure map to her soul—and it did if gray leaf saplings could cure what ailed the village.

When she left the property, Sophia was walking to the greenhouse beyond the willow trees. They waved at each other as Lydia imagined warriors did when they parted ways with their marching orders.

First, secure the Land. Then, heal the villagers.

And perhaps then the elders would see what she was capable of.

The road's loose shells and sandy gravel crunched under her shoes as she hurried to the chapel. By the time her feet hit the cobblestone street, she had forgotten about the new physician and about Sophia's leaving and about Christmas preparations and wanting a second child. None of that mattered now because nothing would matter if she couldn't preserve their very lives.

One hand clutched the notebook and the other skimmed the black iron railing as she climbed the chapel steps. The chapel's two tall, narrow doors were propped open with wooden wedges. The cavernous building smelled like candle wax and old hymnals. She drew in the familiar scent as her eyes adjusted to the dim light. "Connor?"

Her husband's pillar-like silhouette appeared in the office doorway at the far end of the chapel. "Back here, babe."

Her heels clicked on the smooth floorboards as she hurried through the sanctuary. "I must speak with you quickly!"

Before she reached him, a second silhouette moved within the office. "Oh. I didn't know you had a meeting today." Connor opened his hand, and she instinctively took it, but her gaze fixed on the stranger behind him. "Pardon my intrusion."

Connor paused before he spoke, but his unflappable confidence kept his expression neutral. "No need to apologize. You arrived at the perfect time. Jedidiah just got into town and had the trader drop him off here. He says his first order of business is to meet you." As her husband spoke, he drew her into the office with his hand on the small of her back. "Jedidiah Cotter, this is my wife, Dr. Lydia Bradshaw. Lydia, meet your new apprentice."

The young man had curved lips and curious eyes as he gave her a quick nod that was more of a polite bow, his chin dipping to his silken cravat. "It's a pleasure to meet you, Dr. Bradshaw."

If it weren't for the smattering of dust on his handsomely stitched overcoat, she would have guessed the impeccably clad young man had just came from a tailor rather than a long journey on the road. She shook his hand as firmly as any man in the village would have. "The pleasure is mine, I'm sure." Though she kept her tone courteous, she promptly turned her attention to Connor. "May we speak privately?"

A slight lift of Connor's left brow betrayed his displeasure. "If you insist."

"I do. I wouldn't have rushed here with a patient due to the office soon, but the matter is of the utmost importance."

Connor gave her usurper an apologetic look and stepped to the office door. "Excuse us, please."

"Of course." Jedidiah withdrew a folded slip of paper from his breast pocket. "I told my cousin to expect me today as soon as I'd met Missus—or rather—Doctor Bradshaw. Might you direct me to Mark Cotter's farm?"

Lydia let his slip of her title pass without rankling her, but when he named her cousin as his own, her spine stiffened. Everything in her wanted to question him—his familial claim, his education, his former apprenticeship— but she kept her peace while Connor gave him directions.

Jedidiah turned back and said to Lydia, "When would you like me to join you in your medical office?"

Lydia's head spun with the intrusion. "I will let you know."

Connor flicked her a scolding glance, then faced Jedidiah. "Get settled in at the Cotters' tonight and come by our house for dinner tomorrow. We'll work out all the details and you'll get to meet John Colburn."

Lydia's stomach burned as Connor made plans to end her career. While Jedidiah was walking through the chapel to leave, she closed the office door and opened her notebook.

Before she spoke, Connor turned to her, his jaw set tight. "You're wasting your valuable time. The council's decision was final. You must accept it." He blew out a slow breath then lightened his tone. "Besides, didn't you hear Jedidiah? He is Mark's cousin. That means you guys are related. Isn't that reason enough to be cool about this?"

She clapped her notebook between her hands, her fingers curling the cover. "My coming to you has nothing to do with Jedidiah Cotter or the elders' decisions for my patients. I came here because Sophia and I realized the haze might be affecting the gray leaf tree's growth cycle and, in turn, affecting the villagers' health. What's more, if our theory is correct, you can bring one hundred apprentices to the village because we will need them all to fight off the invading armies who are about to discover the Land."

Darkness flitted behind Connor's eyes. "What? Why?"

She opened her abused notebook and read what she'd jotted down during her discussion with Sophia, filling in the gaps in her stunted scribbles with more elaborate thoughts. When she finished, she looked up at Connor.

He had moved closer.

The darkness had vanished from his gaze and only the calm confidence she fell in love with remained. He brushed stray fringe away from her eyes. "Doc, the haze isn't that big of a deal to the gray leaf trees. Bailey said the trees are strong and don't seem to be daunted by a little less daylight."

"A *little* less?" Her voice cracked as her volume increased. "Don't you understand? If the gray leaf molecules indeed help to hide the Land and if their levels have dropped enough to affect everyone's mood, it might also be low enough levels to expose the Land."

He tilted his chin. "No."

"*No* you don't understand or *no* you don't agree?"

"No, I don't think the gray leaf molecules in the air have decreased enough to affect the atmosphere or the people's health. I can still smell the gray leaf trees every morning when I wake up. You're just used to it because you were born here."

She inched her notebook forward as if her scratched out hypothesis were the proof he needed. "But this has to be why I have so many anxious and achy patients."

"You had too many patients before the haze. It wasn't just the Good Springs elders that thought we needed a second physician; it was all the overseers of the Land."

"That's because the overseers of other villages wouldn't understand that the people of Good Springs are most affected by the gray leaf particles, since the main forest is right here outside our village."

He gently squeezed her shoulders and softly slid his hands down her arms. "Justin and Bailey and even her father all agreed with me that the atmospheric anomaly that keeps the Land undetectable to the outside world is more complex than the particles released by the gray leaf trees." He shrugged. "I know you're reaching for anything right now, any reason to stop this change, but you have to let it go."

"I can't when it's about my medical practice and my patients." He wasn't from here; how could he truly understand? She tapped her chest. "These are *my* people being affected, Connor, by the haze and now by you going along with the elder council."

He didn't flinch. "Medicine is good and necessary, but *our* people should be reminded that their peace isn't found in having favorable circumstances but in Christ." He squared his shoulders. "Even if the trees are releasing fewer particles, that isn't the core issue with the anxiety that has swept across the Land."

His words struck her to her core, just as Sophia's had, but from a completely different notion. "Across the Land? Are other villages having the same problems we are... other doctors are facing the same issues I am?"

He pressed his lips together and nodded. "And for every call you have to see a patient with physical anxiety symptoms, your father receives a visit from someone with spiritual symptoms. It's happening in every village. I didn't realize you weren't aware."

"How would I be aware if no one told me? I dash from appointment to appointment all day believing I am the only person holding together a suffering community. You don't tell me anything from the council meetings. Father doesn't tell me anything. And it's all because I am a woman. If Dr. Ashton were still alive and were still the village physician, the elders wouldn't be keeping him in the dark or forcing an apprentice on him."

He shook his head. "It is not because you are a woman, but because Good Springs is the only village without a second physician. You are the youngest doctor in the Land and so you don't have your firstborn in training like all the other physicians."

Little Andrew wanted to be like his daddy, and it looked like he would be their only child. An uninvited tear warmed her cheek. "And I probably won't."

Before she could swipe it away, Connor caught it with his thumb. "You weren't excluded from this decision because you're a woman, but because you aren't an elder. That's the tradition here. You've always insisted that I follow the Land's traditions. Now you must do the same. The overseers of the Land decided each village physician needs a replacement in training. You don't have one and don't have any prospects here, so we found the most qualified for you. Jedidiah was willing to move to Good Springs for life. You have to admit that's admirable."

She wanted to step back to escape his touch, tired of this conversation, tired of his kindness while her heart was full of discontent, but she was too wearied to move. "Fine." She cleared her tight throat and looked out the single-pane office window. "You said Jedidiah would officially complete his apprenticeship under me to gain the village's trust and then be confirmed and titled in Good Springs. So, once he is titled, how will we split my medical practice?"

The crease between his brows deepened. "You're the chief physician here and will be as long as you want the position. You will decide all the details."

Cynicism edged her voice. "At least I have something."

"Doc, you still have everything." He opened his hand to the chair in front of her father's desk. When she sat, he knelt in front of her. "You have Christ and me and Andrew and your family. You have our home and your profession—a job that allows you to receive in trade all the Christmas whatnots you don't have time to make since you're busy saving lives."

He held her gaze. "And I know you're torn between work and home—wanting to keep your practice and grow our family, and you don't feel like either is happening. But this change will help your work, and maybe, just maybe, our infertility is my body, not yours. Or maybe it's both of us. Or neither. Or bad timing." He took her hand and his voice warmed with hope. "It doesn't matter because God will give us exactly what He wants us to have, exactly the work He had prepared us for and exactly the children—or child—He wants us to raise."

The tears were back. She would have a throbbing headache within the hour, but she couldn't make the crying stop. "You're right. I can't shake this feeling that I have a partial family, a partial life, and soon a partial career. I can't be happy about anything, and I don't know why. I'm doing everything right and nothing is working."

"Sometimes, even when we are doing everything right, we aren't thinking right."

Whenever he spoke to her, deep to her soul, whenever her pride finally thinned enough to listen to him, the tears and the headache and the humiliation no longer mattered. She only wanted to absorb his words, his care for her. "I don't know how to fix it."

His grin grew wider. "Good news. I do because I've been through it myself. But if it will only make you angry with me, I won't help you."

A short laugh relaxed her weepy throat. She yanked a handkerchief out of her dress pocket and wiped her eyes while she chuckled at herself, at him, at how well he knew her. "How is it you can make me laugh while I'm crying?"

He shrugged boyishly. "It's a gift."

She stuffed the handkerchief back into her pocket and the last of her pride along with it. "Fine. Tell me what I'm missing."

"This." He stepped to a narrow cupboard in the wall behind her father's desk. It would one day be Connor's desk, then possibly Andrew's.

After shuffling through a shelf of things her father was allowing him to keep in the office, he returned with a small, rectangular present wrapped in tartan cloth, tied with twine. "I know how your dad feels about exchanging Christmas presents, so I was going to give this to you on Christmas Eve if we had time alone. But I think you need it now."

She felt the present's weight and shape. Though she appreciated his gesture, the last thing she had time for was reading a book. "It's only four days to Christmas Eve. We can wait."

"Just open it."

She untied the twine and the cloth fell open, revealing a pocket-sized journal. "It's lovely. Thank you. I can always use another notebook."

He shook his head once. "Nope. This one isn't for work notes or gray leaf research. It is for writing down things you are thankful for. Some people might call it a *gratitude journal.* It's supposed to help you count your blessings. And it's little so you can carry it with you, because I've found it's those times when I'm least prepared that I most need to remind myself of God's faithfulness."

His gift wasn't a reading assignment, yet it felt like homework nonetheless. Connor was ever the good teacher, but she didn't have the luxury of contemplating life lessons at present. She checked her wristwatch and stood. "Thank you. It's very thoughtful. I have to get back to the cottage before my next patient arrives. Sophia is probably still in the greenhouse since we hypothesized that having a potted gray leaf sapling in each home could help people."

He stayed where he was between her and the door without moving, only looking into her eyes, asking her for more than she was ready to give, not to him but to herself. He tapped the little journal. "Learning to be content is a process. Try to write down one thing each day you are grateful for. Just one. Start there." He stepped out of her path. "Soon you will see the truth."

She gave him a quick kiss and smiled. "And the truth shall set me free?"

Seriousness sharpened his gaze as though the words she spouted reflexively held more meaning than she understood. His confident grin returned as he opened the door for her. "Of that, Doc, I have no doubt."

* * *

Instead of retiring to the parsonage for the night, Philip remained in the dining hall after he finished eating dessert. Often when the weather was unsavory, the staff would clean the tables, stoke the fire, and invite the inn's guests to stay for games of cards or charades after the evening meal.

When he first came to Falls Creek, Philip kept his attendance to the game nights sporadic. He neither wanted to cause offense when he preferred an evening of study in the quiet parsonage, nor did he want to stir intrigue when someone requested his private counsel in the chapel. But ever since the haze settled around the Land, the bond of unspoken concern drove him to seek longer times of fellowship, both for his congregants' benefit and for his own.

And with the Vestal siblings seated in the back row of the chapel during this morning's service, he had fought the distraction of curiosity all he could today. Even during dinner, he'd barely heard a word that Naomi or Bailey had said, though they'd sat across the table from him.

It was the three travelers at the next table who had unknowingly commanded his attention, just as they had at every meal for the past few days. He tried to keep his glances at a minimum while the Vestals finished their dessert, but still took notice of their mannerisms, their speech patterns, and their family dynamic.

The thirtyish-year-old Noah Vestal always ate at a steady pace, his shoulders square, spine straight. Such table manners in a man of the field only came from strict childhood discipline. Yet the man's focus was usually fixed on the doorway or the windows more than on his food or his sisters' conversation. His unusual alertness reminded Philip of Connor Bradshaw, who always watched over his shoulder as if an attack were eminent.

However, Noah seemed more like he was eager to leave, even when he'd just arrived.

Across from Noah, Caroline Vestal slowly savored each bite of Sybil's famous cooking. She chatted casually to her younger sister beside her—never of their circumstances or past, but only of books she enjoyed or flowers she hoped to plant in a garden someday. At present, Caroline's chatter was silent while she relished a dish of sugar cream pie. Her low hum of pleasure drew a scowl from her reticent brother.

And then there was Lena, the least in words and in stature of the three. The more Philip observed her, the more he understood why the ancients fell into idol worship. With her rounded cheeks and her innocent eyes, he could easily picture Lena Vestal's image etched into stone and revered as divine. But something in the way she frequently looked to her elder sister made Philip think she would not easily be convinced of such worthiness.

Whether Lena's timidity came from a past wound or from a lifetime of being shaded by two overprotective siblings, Philip couldn't tell. Those were the sorts of details most people weren't around Falls Creek long enough to divulge.

And even he had to admit his thoughts of the Vestals during their short stay were bolstered by more speculation than observation. Something about the family not only captured his attention but also activated his imagination. And in his wonderings he'd found more pleasure than he had in all of life since the haze had appeared.

Perhaps his interest in them was purely that: interest. Their presence gave him something to think about besides the ill-tempered sky. When the Vestal siblings left Falls Creek in a few days, so would his imaginings.

At the back table, a very pregnant Sybil stood from her seat and started to collect the dirty dishes. Isaac quickly pointed her back to her chair and joined Eva in the task. Solo withdrew the plates from his wife's hands and took over for her too. Soon, Bailey and Naomi left Philip's table to help in the kitchen, all while telling Eva and Sybil to relax for a change.

Zeke hopped up from his chair and dashed to the game shelf, skipping half his steps as only a seven-year-old could. He pulled down a basket overflowing with decks of playing cards. "Everybody, let's have a *Pairs* tournament!"

Eva met her son in the middle of the dining room before he could make the adults feel obligated to play a kids' game. "Dearest, our guests might not want to play *Pairs*." Though her voice was aimed at Zeke, her gaze moved to the Vestals. "Let's ask our guests if they want to play *Pairs*."

Noah gave Zeke the first grin Philip had seen on the man's whiskered face, but it was Caroline who spoke up enthusiastically. "Sure, we do! *Pairs* was my favorite game when I was your age."

Noah's dark brow briefly knit then relaxed. No one seemed to notice except Philip.

Eva slipped the basket from Zeke's flimsy grip and smiled at her son. "Excellent. *Pairs* it is. Good idea, Zeke."

Zeke whooped with excitement through his missing-toothed grin. "Let's start the tournament with girls against boys."

Eva scanned the room. "Anyone object?"

Caroline smiled at Zeke. "Sounds like fun!"

Lena smiled at the boy too, but only after her sister had.

Eva and Zeke planned out the match while the four in the kitchen clanked dishes as they washed and dried and stacked. Soon, everyone was back in the dining hall, obeying Eva's directions to their new seating arrangements.

Sybil rubbed her belly and scowled as she slowly lowered her swollen frame to her assigned seat. Philip moved to the seat where he was told, but didn't hear the rest of Eva's instructions as his attention was drawn to Sybil's change in demeanor.

When Isaac took his assigned place next to him, Philip leaned over. "Is your wife quite all right?"

Isaac's gaze shot across the room to Sybil. At that moment, she was chatting happily to Caroline. Isaac pursed his lips. "She looks fine to me. Why?"

"She seemed ill at ease, I suppose."

"Probably just ready for the baby to come. The physician that was here the other day, Jedidiah Cotter, checked her out. Said that she and the baby are as they should be."

"Good to hear. I look forward to welcoming the first baby born into our church and—" Philip instantly forgot about everyone and everything else in the room, for Lena Vestal was assigned the seat across from him.

Claudia sat in the fourth chair at their table and tucked her silver hair behind her ear. "Looks like I'm playing against you, Isaac."

The older woman and Isaac both chuckled, the bond of extended family erasing the disparity in their ages.

Philip met Lena's gaze across the narrow table, seeing in her hazel eyes golden flecks that hinted at the warmth trapped behind them.

There went his imagination again.

He picked up the deck of cards that waited between them. "Shall I shuffle?"

Lena only nodded, bobbing the flyaway strands of loose, light brown curls that framed her face.

Eva breezed past and tapped Philip's shoulder. "Yes, men shuffle, then ladies deal. Winner plays the other winner at their table for round two."

Philip handed Lena the shuffled deck. "Zeke beats me every time we play this game. I've yet to determine if I lack skill or if the boy has devised a clever scheme."

Lena grinned then gave the cards one more shuffle, watching him instead of the cards in her hands. "I've never been much good at cards, either. My brother and sister get competitive when we play games, but not me."

At last! A hint of her personality.

His pulse increased with the first whiff of truth divulged by this mysterious woman. He glanced at Claudia and Isaac to make sure they were engaged in their own conversation. Claudia was grilling Isaac on his duties during the birthing process, emphasizing that as the midwife of all births at the inn for almost fifty years, she would expect his complete cooperation and for him to remain courageous for his wife's sake.

Satisfied they wouldn't listen, Philip picked up his cards, mindlessly selected one, and placed it on the table. "If not games, what do you prefer to do with your leisure time?"

She laid a card atop his and slid the pair to her stack to claim the point. Her lips pulled to one side while she thought. "Lacemaking, I guess. And writing."

"What kind of writing?"

A faint blush colored her cheeks. "Anything to practice my penmanship. I compose little poems and the like. Nonsense, really."

"I'm sure it isn't nonsense."

"Don't be." As soon as the words came from her mouth, she tucked her chin and stared at her cards.

Philip could feel a glare from the next table over. He stole a glance, expecting it to be from her brother, but it was Caroline who raised an eyebrow at him. She held it there until Leonard claimed a pair and returned her attention to their game. Her congenial smile for the elderly Leonard quickly softened her face.

Lena said something under her breath.

"Pardon?"

She pointed to the card she'd laid down. "Do you have a match?"

"Oh, sorry. No."

"Don't be sorry. We're supposed to be competing against each other, remember?"

A chuckle escaped his throat, surprised by her humor. She might be reserved, but there was certainly more to her than he had imagined.

But had she formed an opinion of him?

He left an easy card on the table for her to win a point. "What did you think of the chapel service today? Much different from the Northcrest church services?"

The cards in her hands went very still.

When she didn't speak, he leaned in. "That different?"

She kept her sweet voice equally quiet. "In two ways, sir."

"Pray, what were they?"

Her gaze bounced from her brother to her sister and back to him. She continued her turn with the cards. "One difference was the size of the crowd."

"Ah, yes. There are more than a dozen in the pews in Northcrest, I presume."

She grinned. "Yes, many more."

"And the other?"

She glanced at her sister, who was no longer watching them. "You seemed... your sermon, that is, seemed as if you have a passion for the Scriptures. I felt like you spent time pouring over the verses out of a love for God's Word and not—"

A cry of pain resounded from the other side of the dining hall, turning every head. Sybil splayed both hands over her belly and sucked in an audible breath. She stood from her chair so forcefully it screeched across the floor behind her. Water puddled between her feet. "It's happening!"

Next to Philip, Isaac shot up and dashed to his wife, leaving a scattering of playing cards across the table and his chair.

Sybil clutched her middle and groaned with wide eyes, another contraction yanking a cry from her lungs.

Isaac's face was almost as flushed as his wife's. "Let's get you home, love. Quickly. Solo, the wagon."

Claudia hurried across the dining hall as best as her arthritic knees could carry her. "She won't make a wagon ride in this condition. Take her up to a room."

Eva was already in her office, grabbing the key to an available guest room. "Isaac, take her up to Room Four."

She pointed at the wet floor as Isaac ushered Sybil out of the dining hall. "Naomi, get a mop, please."

The room was a flurry of angst and anticipation, all eyes on Sybil. She waddled to the doorway, dripping and panting all the way. Before she made it to the corridor, Isaac scooped her into his arms and carried her up the stairs. Eva was close behind them.

Claudia held the rail, taking each step slowly. "Just breathe, dear. You'll be fine. Remember what we talked about. Isaac, you breathe too."

Once the birthing party ascended the steps, those left stood in silence. The three Vestals exchanged uneasy glances.

Solo pulled Zeke close to his side. "Aunt Sybil will be just fine, partner."

Leonard patted Zeke's arm. "Course she will. The baby too." The older man returned to his seat. "Won't be coming for a while yet. These things take time. What do you say we finish our game?"

Zeke shrugged and looked up at Solo. "Is that all right?"

Solo's expression held the same uncertainty as all the adults in the room, and the same bravery. "Sure. Claudia and Eva will take good care of Sybil. And the good Lord will let what comes natural to women just happen, right Reverend?"

When Solo looked at Philip, everyone else did too.

He hated being called such titles. In his estimation only Christ was to be revered, but this was no time for such discussions. He offered a sure grin, first to Zeke, then Solo, Leonard, Naomi, Bailey, and then to the Vestal siblings, saving Lena for last. "Of course, He will." He opened his hand to the table. "Let's pray for Sybil and the baby, and then continue Zeke's *Pairs* tournament while we await the birth of his very first cousin."

CHAPTER SEVEN

Thick cloud cover blocked the last hours of sunlight, turning a miserable day into a cold, stormy night, unlike any Christmas Eve Lydia had ever experienced. After the year she had endured—the year the world had endured—nothing should surprise her, especially the weather. At least, her schedule had been manageable today, and the patient currently in her office would recover quickly.

There. She *was* grateful for something. Perhaps she should write that in the journal Connor gave her four days ago… when she got around to it.

If she got around to it.

While her patient's husband readied his wagon for the blustery drive home, Lydia sat at her desk, making notes in her medical chart. Seventeen stitches closed the woman's wound. A course of gray leaf tea removed her pain and quieted her hysteria from a kitchen accident involving a fillet knife.

Light snores came from the patient cot as the gray leaf medicine deepened its hold.

Lydia's new apprentice, Jedidiah, was outside helping to raise the canvas cover on the patient's wagon. The young man's temporary absence allowed Lydia her first moments in the office without him since Monday. Sophia had just gotten married and left Lydia, and Jedidiah had already filled the medical cottage with an unmistakable male presence.

And he combed his hair too often.

Maybe he had come to Good Springs to look for a wife. Lydia doubted he would find an eligible match in a patient, so his frequent grooming only wasted precious time. When she was an apprentice, she studied medical textbooks between patient visits. Granted, Dr. Ashton often went days between appointments. Thus far, Jedidiah had eagerly observed her treat one patient after another.

Still, she might suggest he study more and preen less.

As of yet, she hadn't suggested anything. Suggesting led to teaching, and teaching led to training. And if she trained him, she would have to title him, thereby validating him as her responsibility. Every other professional in the Land chose their own apprentices; hers had been forced upon her. It wasn't that she didn't approve of Jedidiah Cotter as a person; she didn't approve of this arrangement.

The cottage door opened abruptly, and the wind swept it to the wall with a clatter. Pounding rain drenching the doormat. Jedidiah didn't bother wiping his polished boots or closing the door before crossing the medical office. Without a word, he scooped Lydia's plump and drowsy patient from the cot as if the middle-aged woman weighed no more than a lamb.

A raucous snore came from the patient's gaping mouth as Jedidiah turned sideways to carry her out. The rain had flattened his coiffed hair into a dripping mop. If he'd been Lydia's younger brother or one of Bethany's friends, she would have thought him heroically adorable in that moment. She shut the door behind them, then released a chuckle as she watched out the window.

So perhaps it wouldn't be all bad having a male apprentice around the office. She certainly couldn't have asked Sophia to carry a dozing patient to a wagon in the pouring rain. And come to think of it, she hadn't asked Jedidiah to do it either.

Lightning cracked the sky overhead as he settled the patient in the back of the covered wagon, but Jedidiah didn't flinch.

Maybe she had judged him too harshly.

When he wasn't fidgeting with his dapper cravat or straightening his starched cuffs, he did seem to possess the natural disposition of a physician. He was genuinely curious about each patient's symptoms, respectful in his questions, and quick to assist Lydia, though she'd yet to assign him even the smallest task.

Even so, being motivated didn't mean he would be able to handle any medical situation. After all, she'd stitched this patient's wound, just as she'd treated all the other patients this week. Most healthy young men in the village could carry a person if necessary.

Jedidiah would have to do more than show initiative before she allowed him to treat her patients; he would have to prove his medical skills.

Connor disagreed. He wanted her to trust Jedidiah with her practice so she could take Christmas day off work. Oh, how lovely it would be to spend her favorite holiday in the Colburn house with her family—laughing with her husband, cooking her father's favorite dishes, and playing with Andrew!

But not at the expense of the villagers' health.

What if Jedidiah couldn't properly set a broken bone? Or extract a foreign object? Just yesterday, she'd had to remove glass from a man's foot, and the day before, a bean from a child's nostril. Did Jedidiah have the skill for such cases?

And if tomorrow was the day the elderly Mr. Vestal died, she would have to go out to the Vestal orchard to certify his death, anyway. There could be no such thing as a *day off* for her. Hadn't her last attempt proven that?

The door opened again, and this time Jedidiah stayed on the doormat while rain dripped from his jacket. The storm had sucked the elegance from his manicured appearance and left only a young man who was soaking wet and far from home.

For an instant, the situation smacked of taking in a stray dog; if she gave him any attention, it would be difficult to get him to leave. Yet, he reminded her less of a stray dog needing a home and more of the feral cats she tried luring to the barn, knowing the more cats there were around to hunt vermin, the less trouble there would be with pests.

Perhaps a second physician would benefit Good Springs.

And her.

She pulled a fluffy towel from the cupboard beside the worktable and carried it to him. "Leave your boots there and hang your coat on the rack, then go upstairs to dry off."

He glanced up the staircase and back at her, a grin creasing the corners of his eyes. "I carried one patient out and now I'm allowed up the sacred stairs?"

Her throat issued one short laugh. She could see why Connor liked him; her husband appreciated anyone with a sense of humor.

If she had been too guarded of the cottage, it was because her father had built it for her and for her medical practice. She cherished the time she had lived in the private rooms upstairs, but she didn't need to tell Jedidiah that. "It isn't sacred. Go dry off. Just... be quick about it."

He wiped his face with the towel and took the stairs two at a time.

As she capped her pen and filed the day's medical charts in her desk drawer, she considered leaving Jedidiah in the office for the remainder of the evening while she went to the house to be with her family on Christmas Eve. If it went well, she might allow him to man the office tomorrow. He had already said the holiday made no difference to him.

Maybe Connor had been right... again.

Maybe she could trust someone with her work while she enjoyed Christmas. And then maybe also on Andrew's birthday. And then never miss a church service or the family luncheon at the Foster farm each Sunday afternoon.

It had been so long...

Sentiment wrestled sensibility in her mind. She planted both hands on her desk and drew a long breath. She was only thinking this way because it was Christmas Eve and she wanted desperately to be with her family, to be like all the other village women and bake and sing and decorate.

But how could she hand over her practice to someone who was trained by another physician and might not be able to care for her patients?

She needed proof, any proof of his aptitude.

Wind howled between the window panes as Jedidiah descended the stairs. His hair was sleek with fresh comb lines, but only his gray waistcoat remained over his white, buttoned-up shirt. His cravat was missing from his collar. "I hung my jacket in the washroom to dry. If my appearance is unacceptable, I can fetch my other suit from home."

She dismissed his concern with a flick of her wrist. "You would only drench yourself again while riding back from the Cotters' farm."

"Some storm out there, isn't it?"

"I prefer a rainstorm to the snow the villagers had predicted for Christmas."

He whistled one low note. "Snow at Christmas? What a year! My parents said they've never seen such weather in Stonehill in their lifetime."

At the mention of his parents and village, a ping of guilt tightened her chest. No, she had not given the young man a chance. She opened her hand to the chair beside her desk. "Have a seat. Tell me about your training in Stonehill. How did you secure the apprenticeship there?"

Pleasant surprise brightened his eyes as he sat. "Much obliged. Well, our overseer arranged my training. My brother is to inherit our family's salt mine, and my teachers thought my academic ability made me more suited to medicine or teaching than to mining. After Doctor Ashton—our Doctor Ashton—had trained and titled his son, he told our village council he would train another physician. So, they recommended me for the apprenticeship."

She studied his unwrinkled face. He couldn't be much over twenty. "When was that?"

"Six years ago."

"A six-year apprenticeship?"

He nodded. "Doctor Ashton had me study medical texts for two years and complete his written exams before he allowed me to observe him with his patients. I spent three years with him every day and assisted him with every patient. Only in the past year did he allow me to treat patients surgically, perform wound dressing, sutures, extract teeth, and so forth."

"Pray, how old are you?"

"Twenty and nine next month."

So, this baby-faced man was not only a year older than her, but also had more training in his apprenticeship than she had in hers?

Connor might have mentioned these things when he introduced Jedidiah. Then again, she hadn't been eager to learn anything about him, so she probably wouldn't have listened anyway.

Thunder rattled the cottage, and they both looked at the door. How she wanted to be in the cozy kitchen, cooking for Connor and Andrew right now! Christmas came but once a year.

She studied Jedidiah's profile until he returned his attention to her. Her sentimental heart was gaining victory over her sensible brain. "In your apprenticeship, were you often left alone to treat patients?"

"Yes, often."

"And during those times, did you ever find yourself in... negative circumstances?"

He leaned forward a degree. "Doctor, there are no negative circumstances, only unique opportunities."

"I see." His answer amazed her, but she dared not show it. She stood to maintain her authority. "And during those *unique opportunities*, did you find you were always able to give the patient complete and thorough care?"

"Always."

The tightness inside her chest loosened. Perhaps in this case, the sentimental choice was also the sensible choice. "If I am to determine your readiness to be titled, I must give you the opportunity to do the work. Would you feel comfortable with—"

The clatter of horse and wagon rumbled onto the property, then halted outside the cottage. They both dashed to the door. Jedidiah reached it first, but only opened it and allowed Lydia to exit first.

She expected to see her patient returning, her mind speculating reasons. Instead, a hulking trader's wagon filled the space between the cottage and the kitchen door of the Colburn house.

Revel Roberts clambered down from the back of the wagon with a little boy draped in his arms. "Dr. Bradshaw! Quick! Their wagon turned over into a ditch outside the village. They were trapped for hours. We just came upon them. They all need your attention. Hurry!"

Rain pelted her face as she took the child from him. The boy was about Andrew's age, his body shaking, his skin clammy. She held him close and glanced inside the wagon before she carried the boy into the office. When the light reached his face, she raised each eyelid to check his pupils.

Before she could lay his tiny body on the patient cot, Jedidiah burst through the doorway. "Where is your stretcher?"

She lifted her chin at the narrow closet near the supply cabinet. "In there. How many children are there?"

"One more. A girl." He yanked the rolled-up stretcher from the cabinet. "This is for their mother. She's about to issue a baby before its time."

Revel lumbered into the office, carrying a bearded man about the same size as himself. He lowered the unconscious man to the patient cot. "You'll need more beds."

Her arms burned with the weight of the shivering boy. "There are several cots in the barn. Get Connor. He's in the house. He knows where to find them."

Revel rushed out the door just before Jedidiah and the trader inched inside with a grimacing mother on the stretcher. She had both hands pressed to her pregnant belly, her cheeks puffing with forced exhales, her forehead scratched from the accident.

As they lowered the stretcher to the rug in the middle of the office floor, Revel returned with a little girl who clung to his neck, sobbing. He knelt beside the girl's mother. "Stay here with your mama, Rosie. I have to get more cots. You will be all right. I promise Doctor Bradshaw will take good care of you."

Lydia laid the little boy on the rug near his mother, then gave the girl a quick scan and estimated her to be about six years of age. Though red-faced from crying and soaked to the bone, she didn't appear injured. "Are you hurt?"

The girl shook her head.

The mother took one hand off her belly and pulled her son close to her. "He wasn't hurt badly when the wagon went off the road, but we all got soaked in the rain. He's chilled to the bone. Won't come to properly."

Jedidiah was at the patient cot with his fingers on the father's neck and his eyes on his pocket watch. "His pulse is steady. Lacerations to his face and arms." He lifted the man's eyelids. "Possibly concussed."

The mother gasped from labor pains, then spoke through clenched teeth. "My husband had us ride in the back while he drove in the rain. He was on the bench alone when we rolled. Those traders said they found him thrown from the wagon." She let out a groan that would curdle a lion's blood and grabbed her abdomen. "My baby isn't due for a month!"

Lydia raised her voice to speak to Jedidiah over the mother's groaning and the girl's weeping. "He must have a dose of gray leaf vapor at once. Have you ever administered it?"

Jedidiah pointed to the mother. "No, but I've delivered several babies."

"Very well. You tend to her while I revive him."

Lydia grabbed a vial of gray leaf vapor and a syringe from the medicine cabinet over her worktable, then took two towels from the cupboard and gave the girl one. "Remove your wet clothes and wrap up in this until we find you some dry clothes. Sit there by the fireplace to warm up."

She set the gray leaf aside and stripped the tiny boy's wet clothes and wrapped him in a towel too. Jedidiah was at the cupboard drawing out a pillow for the mother. Lydia raised her free hand. "I need one here too." She propped up the shivering boy by his sister, and thanked God her own little boy was safe inside their warm house.

Connor and Revel returned with extra cots and helped Jedidiah situate the mother and children, while Lydia forced gray leaf vapor into the father's airway. After one natural inhale, he coughed and sucked in the rest with a jolt. The room went momentarily still as everyone watched the injured man open his eyes.

The laboring mother let out a deep wail that sent her daughter back to crying. Then she pointed at Connor and Revel. "I don't want an audience. I'm having a baby!"

Lydia nodded at her husband and Revel. "Thank you."

Connor winked at her with a half grin that let her know he was more impressed with her ability than worried for the injured family.

The man's breathing stabilized and the gray leaf medicine quickly lulled him to a deep sleep. Lydia checked the little boy again. He'd stopped shivering, and the color had returned to his cheeks.

As she went back to the father's cot to stitch his wounds, the mother grasped her hand. Between pants, she asked, "How is Joseph?"

"Your husband?"

She shook her sweaty head. "No, my son."

Lydia patted the woman's white-knuckled hand. "He will be fine. He's sleeping."

"And my husband—" A scream of labor pain ended her question.

Jedidiah lifted the sheet draped over the mother's lower half. "Mrs. Owens, it's time to push."

The mother's howls swallowed the little girl's whimpers, and while Lydia stitched the father's lacerations, Jedidiah helped deliver a premature but lively baby boy.

CHAPTER EIGHT

L ydia checked her wristwatch by the glow of her office's fireplace. Almost four in the morning. Christmas morning.

The two Owens children were asleep, snuggly tucked under warm blankets, sharing a single cot as little Rosie requested. Lydia had given them each half a child's dosage of gray leaf medicine as a precaution.

Mrs. Owens was dozing between feedings with her new baby boy beside her cot in a rudimentary basinet—a laundry basket lined with a folded quilt. The exhausted mother had fallen asleep with one hand gripping the basket's handle, and there it remained.

Lydia expected Mr. Owens' external wounds to heal quickly. She would have to assess his internal condition by daylight once he could articulate his symptoms.

She stepped quietly to her desk. Jedidiah was sitting in the chair beside it, making notes by the low light of her oil lamp. His disheveled hair hung over his forehead, his sleeves were rolled to his elbows, and his well-stitched waistcoat was draped over the stair rail.

She pulled her chair out from under her desk. "You should go home to rest."

Before she sat, he stood and whispered. "If it's all right with you, I want to stay and observe them for the remainder of the evening."

She tapped her wristwatch. "It's almost morning."

"Even so," he looked at the mother and the baby, "I prefer to stay in case they need me... in case you need me."

He certainly possessed a physician's best qualities—the qualities her village deserved. After his thorough and compassionate work through the night, she would have granted him the title of *Doctor* on the spot if the village elders were here to witness it. Thankfully, her sensibility overtook her sentiment in this case. Jedidiah needed a few months of oversight before he was titled and autonomous, just as she and the village needed time to accept him as one of their own. No doubt remained in her heart that they would all approve of him in a short time. That time started now.

She pointed at his notebook. "Would you like to complete their medical charts for me?"

His eyes shone. "Their official charts?"

She nodded.

"I'd be honored, Doctor."

She covered a yawn as she slid a stack of blank charts she'd prepared.

He lifted his chin at the patients. "They will all sleep past sunrise. I can stay if you wish to go inside and get some rest."

Despite her fatigue, a bubble of joy warmed her heart. She didn't need sleep, couldn't sleep. Not now. She had a cottage full of patients and a household soon to awaken to Christmas morning. But what enlivened her most was knowing she had a capable physician she could trust with her practice whenever she needed to enjoy other blessings in her life.

She pushed her chair back under her desk. "Very well. I will be back by seven. The kitchen door is unlocked if—"

"I will come to you immediately if there is any change."

"Excellent. Thank you, Jedidiah." She wrapped her woolen shawl over her shoulders. "Good job last night."

He nodded once as she closed the office door.

Her feet hit the flagstones, expecting a quick jaunt in the rain from the cottage to the house, yet she halted. The storm had passed. Instead of leaving the temperature cold and the air foggy, a warm breeze softly blew in from the nearby ocean. Stars danced in the sky above, and light from the perfect oval moon flooded the yard.

She loosened her grip on her shawl. The predawn air felt like it used to on a summer morning in the Land.

It felt like Christmas.

The lamp was still burning on the kitchen table, its flame turned as low as possible by someone knowing she would be out all night. Either her father or Connor. The parlor was empty, as she'd hoped it would be. She didn't want Connor sleeping in an armchair, waiting up for her. He likely knew better since he saw the state of her patients.

She peeked down the hallway. The doors to both the guest room and Aunt Isabella's old bedroom were closed. Revel usually stayed with them when he went through the village on his messenger route. Apparently, the heroic trader who saved the Owens family from their overturned wagon had stayed the night too.

Between the six people in the house and the five in the cottage, breakfast needed to be plentiful. She shuffled back into the kitchen and increased the lamp's flame. The countertops were lined with covered dishes. Word of her situation must have spread through the village last night. She drew a slow breath to stop the joyful tears that warmed behind her eyes, and whispered, "Thank you, Lord, for my village."

Her fingers trailed the banister as she ascended the stairs, stepping as lightly as possible. Andrew's bedroom door was ajar, and moonlight filtered through the lacy curtains over the window, spreading a dappled pattern over the floor and the bed. What was once the nursery now had small wooden blocks and toy trinkets scattered across the rug.

Andrew slept on his belly with his arms splayed out on each side, his mouth slightly open. Though nothing could wake her sweet boy when he was so deep in sleep, she quietly crept into the room and knelt by his bed. He would likely be her only child, but that didn't sadden her anymore. Andrew was safe and healthy, smart and energetic. And he was hers.

Connor had been correct: God gave them the child He wanted them to raise. It didn't matter that her mother had borne five children by her age, or that her younger sister was expecting twins, or that every other woman in the village seemed to have more babies than cribs. She would never again see the responsibility of motherhood as anything less than a privilege, whether she had one child or ten. She softly kissed his cheek and silently thanked the Lord for allowing her to be a mother.

Her father's door was closed, as was the door to her and Connor's bedroom. No matter how deeply her husband was sleeping, he might shoot out of bed the second he heard any sharp noise.

She turned the glass knob as incrementally as the minute hand on a clock and tiptoed to her dresser, where she had thoughtlessly abandoned his thoughtful gift.

Connor stirred under the quilt. "Hey, babe. You okay?"

"Yes, perfectly fine. Just getting something. Go back to sleep."

"Are your patients okay?"

She sat on his side of the bed and stroked his hair. "They will be."

"Did she have a boy or girl?"

"A boy. He and his mother are doing well. The other children are fine. They're sleeping. I expect Mr. Owens to recover."

Connor rolled onto his side. "Revel said Mr. Vestal's heir is on his way to Good Springs. Noah Vestal is his name. He is bringing his two sisters with him. They will take care of Mr. Vestal while Noah tends the orchard."

She yawned before she responded. "Mr. Vestal doesn't have much longer."

"They know." He tugged on her sleeve. "Come to bed."

"No. It's almost morning. I only came upstairs to get this." She lifted the journal even though Connor's eyes were closed. "I must go downstairs in case Jedidiah needs me."

"You need sleep."

"I'll lie down in the parlor if I have to." She kissed his forehead. "Merry Christmas, love."

"Merry Christmas."

"Thank you for the journal. I will fill it with as many blessings as I can think of. I have so much to be grateful for."

"I'm glad you like it."

"I wish I had a present for you."

He gave her hip a squeeze. "You are my present."

His sleepy charm made her smile. She kissed him again. "I'll be downstairs."

As she opened the door, he whispered, "I love you."

The gratitude in her heart grew, not simply because of his love for her, but for all that he was, for all that God had given them, and for this life they were allowed to live together. "I love you, too."

She pressed the empty journal to her heart as she padded back down to the kitchen table. A click of the lamp's dial increased its flame so she could write. As her thankfulness poured from her heart to the page, her spirit lifted. The petty grievances that had weighed her down had also blinded her to all the goodness in her life—the goodness that abounded despite her circumstances and those of the world, within her homeland and without.

She lost track of time as she filled the journal's pages. A rooster in the yard behind the medical cottage blasted his battle cry against the coming day at what would normally be first light. Though she hoped the sound didn't disturb her patients, it didn't pull her attention away from her writing.

The arrhythmic shuffle of her husband's early-morning footsteps swished across the floorboards as he entered the kitchen. His short, black hair was messy, his threadbare white t-shirt wrinkled. He lumbered straight to the sink and filled the kettle. "Coffee?"

"Already?"

"It's six."

"Sure." She tapped her pen to the page. "You were right about this... about everything, really."

He sent a grin over his shoulder as he lit the stove's firebox. "Everything, huh?"

"Yes." This time she was behind him before he expected it. She wrapped her arms around him and laid her head against his strong back. "You knew exactly what I needed."

He turned and drew her to his chest. "And?"

"And I have everything I need."

"Yes, we do."

"Even food for our guests on Christmas." She pulled away to look up at him in the lamplight. "But I didn't do any of the things a wife in the Land traditionally does at Christmas. Do you mind that I didn't prepare any of your favorites dishes this year?"

The shadow deepened between his brows. "Are you kidding? It didn't even cross my mind. You know why?"

"Hm?"

"We both have particular callings. Unique callings. We don't live like everyone else, so our lives won't look like anyone else's."

As he spoke, soft morning light warmed the east-facing window. For a second, she thought she might be dreaming. Her heart pounded hard once in her chest. "Look!"

Connor didn't move a muscle, but his eyes bulged.

He saw it too.

She wasn't dreaming!

She hurried him to the kitchen door and stepped outside without her shoes. The flagstones cooled her feet, but every inch of her body warmed as they watched the sun's first light glow through the trees that stood between the Colburn property and the shore. A laugh burst from her throat. "It's gone! The haze is gone!"

Connor hugged her and swooped her in a happy circle outside the kitchen door. He gripped her hand, and they backed across the yard until rays from the first real sunrise in months hit their faces.

He scoured the sky in every direction and let out a whoop of joy. "It's clear in every direction. Hallelujah!"

John appeared in the doorway, wearing his trousers and an undershirt, tugging on his boots. "What is happening?"

Andrew squeezed past him and ran outside in his pajamas. "It's Christmas!"

Lydia scooped up her little boy and pointed at the clear horizon. "Look! That ugly haze is gone. We expected it to linger for another year at least, but it's gone. Isn't it wonderful!"

John had both hands raised and tears welling in his eyes as he watched the sunrise. "Thank you, Lord!"

Connor pulled Lydia to his side, and when he did, Andrew instantly moved from her arms to his. That didn't bother her anymore either. Her son had a godly father, and he wanted to be close to him. That was more than she could have asked or imagined. She looked up at Connor's trustworthy eyes. "What a wonderful Christmas gift!"

John's joyful voice broke with emotion. "Amen!"

Connor held Lydia close to him with one arm and their son securely in the other. "God always gives the best presents."

Life might never be the same as it once was, but it was exactly as it was supposed to be. She gazed at the beautifully clear sky and drew in a long breath of warm air. "Amen!"

* * *

Normally, Sybil would play a joyful chorus on the piano at the end of the service while everyone stood to leave. Nothing was normal about this morning's early Christmas service.

When Philip ended his closing prayer, the chapel remained silent. Sybil stayed seated on the pew next to Isaac and cradled her precious three-day-old baby. As Philip passed the happy family on his way to open the chapel door, the new mother offered him a tired smile. "Maybe by Sunday I'll be able to play."

A smile tugged on Philip's lips in return. "Take all the time you need."

Though he'd already established that the tradition of the Falls Creek church would be to have Easter and Christmas services end at sunrise, something else felt different today. It wasn't just the silence. As he pulled the chapel door open, a ray of early morning sunlight poured through the crack in the door, growing into a flood of light.

Philip's breath caught as he stepped out of the chapel and into the first true sunrise he'd seen in months. "Hallelujah!"

He moved to the side of the door to shake the hand of each of the attendants before they descended the steps, as was his custom, but instead of an orderly line of solemn faces, there was a scurry inside the chapel. "Sunlight!"

"It's gone! That terrible haze is gone."

Zeke dashed out of the door first, flew past Philip, and jumped down the chapel's three stone steps. "Where'd that big cloud go?"

Solo followed his stepson outside. "Back to the devil where it belongs." He widened his eyes at Philip. "Sorry, Reverend."

Philip let it all go, too overwhelmed by the warmth of the orange sunlight bathing his face. With everyone eager to get outside, the first few to exit didn't stop to shake his hand or to thank him for the service. It didn't matter. That wasn't why he was here.

The residents of the inn gathered in clusters on the road between the inn and the chapel. Solo had his arms around Eva while they watched Zeke make long shadows, dancing in the sunlight. Leonard and Claudia hobbled down the steps one at a time, both telling each other to use the rail for balance. Naomi stayed close behind them with a concerned hand outstretched. Isaac held the newborn in the crook of his arm, while Sybil watched the baby more than the sunrise.

Bailey stopped in front of Philip and looked to the east. "So cool!" Then she smiled at him. "Pretty awesome, huh?"

He shook her hand. "I wouldn't call the sun *cool*, but I agree the sunrise is *pretty* and its power *awesome*."

She chuckled and walked on. "Yeah, well. The plants in the greenhouse will be happy."

"As are we all," Caroline said as she led her siblings out of the chapel. "Thank you for inviting us this morning." She pointed to the east. "It looks like God answered your prayers."

"He always answers, Miss Vestal. This time He answered in the affirmative."

Noah shook his hand next. "Good service. Thanks."

"My pleasure."

Lena walked outside last, the sun glinting off the golden specks in her hazel eyes. Instead of watching her brother and sister, who were already descending the chapel steps, she stopped and looked directly at Philip. "I very much enjoyed your teaching. I'd never heard a sermon about grace on Christmas. It's usually about Mary and shepherds and angels. You made much sense, though, and gave me plenty to be thankful for."

Caroline and Noah stopped near the road and talked quietly. They didn't look back for their younger sister, but neither did they leave her behind.

Lena pointed at the sun. "I think I missed sunrises more than sunsets. How about you?"

Philip let his vision trail along her delicate arm to her pointing finger, but didn't look at the sun as it was now fully risen, bright and glorious, and impossible for the human eye to withstand. "I missed both in equal measure."

In his peripheral vision, Philip could see everyone else crossing the yard to go into the inn. The family always exchanged gifts and sang carols after the service and then enjoyed a Christmas brunch in the dining hall. Philip was usually eager to join them, and he would, but for the moment he was alone and face-to-face with the woman who in one short week had captured his attention and stirred his heart.

At once, he remembered what a trader had left for him last week. He gestured toward the parsonage with a casual thumb. "Miss Vestal—"

"Lena."

"Lena, I recently received a package of exquisite writing paper. I recall you saying you enjoy writing and practicing your penmanship. If I sent half of the paper with you when you leave here tomorrow, would you consider corresponding with me?"

Her delicate lips parted slightly, then curved. "Why, yes. I would very much enjoy that."

His anxious fingertips tingled. "Excellent."

"I'm not sure I will write anything you'll find worth reading, but I look forward to it anyhow."

His hand raised to touch her arm but stopped, careful not to give her older siblings offense. "I suspect I will find every word you write worth reading."

Her smile broadened and she broke their gaze, her hesitance seeming more from chastity than timidity. Yes, there was much more to Lena Vestal than he first imagined.

EPILOGUE

After a night spent at the overseer's house in Woodland and then a night of camping alongside the road, Caroline Vestal blew out a long breath when their wagon passed the first farmhouse on the outskirts of Good Springs. "Whew! We finally made it! You don't know how many times I wanted to ask you: *are we there yet?*"

Noah rolled his eyes at her. "Don't be such a baby."

"Hey, can't a girl be glad to get off a wagon and maybe, just maybe, have her own bedroom for the first time in twenty years?"

"You complain too much. We're lucky to be alive. And even luckier to be inheriting a home and an orchard from these people." He looked back through the opening in the wagon cover. "Lena's still asleep."

"Oh, I should wake her so she can see the village for the first time with us."

Noah took one hand off the reins to stop her. "Before you do, we need to talk."

Now it was her turn to roll her eyes. "Here goes the big brother speech. I'm twenty-eight years old, you know."

"Yes, I do know. I also know how you get when you're all excited to meet people."

"I can behave myself here. Father and Mother made sure of that."

"And we should be grateful."

"I am."

He adjusted his hat, making himself look like a Wild West cowboy. They used to get a kick out of that when they were teenagers, but the older he got, the more serious he became about fitting in to this culture. "We need this farm, Caroline. The orchard will be my livelihood and yours and Lena's too, at least as long as you're under my roof."

She chortled. "Your roof? Um, whatever, Dad."

He sighed. "Just be cool, okay?"

"I will be. I'm only myself around you."

"Lucky me."

She play hit him in the arm and made him grin. "There's my brother."

The sky was gloriously clear and the air warm, as it should be a week after the summer solstice. She gazed out across the sheep-dotted hills to the west, then breathed in the salty-sweet breeze blowing from the east. "I just want to make some friends here, have some fun for once. Maybe I'll have a best friend."

Playful sarcasm filled his voice. "Wow, a best friend *and* your own room. You'll be the talk of the yacht club."

"You know it." She chuckled easily, reminders of a lost childhood not hurting like they used to.

As their new village came into view, she turned to awaken Lena. Noah stopped her once more and whispered, "Whatever you do, just remember, no one can find out where we are really from."

Thank you for reading my book. I'm so glad you went on this journey with me. More Uncharted stories await you! Are you ready for the adventure?

I know it's important for you to enjoy these wholesome, inspirational stories in your favorite format, so I've made sure all of my books are available in ebook, paperback, and large print versions.

Below is a quick description of each story so that you can determine which books to order next…

The Uncharted Series
A hidden land settled by peaceful people ~ The first outsider in 160 years

The Land Uncharted (#1)
Lydia's secluded society is at risk when an injured fighter pilot's parachute carries him to her hidden land.

Uncharted Redemption (#2)
When vivacious Mandy is forced to depend on strong, silent Levi, she must learn to accept tender love from the one man who truly knows her.

Uncharted Inheritance (#3)
Bethany and Everett belong together, but when a mysterious man arrives in the Land, everything changes.

Christmas with the Colburns (#4)
When Lydia faces a gloomy holiday in the Colburn house, an unexpected gift brightens her favorite season.

Uncharted Grace (#12)
Caroline and Jedidiah must overcome their shattered
pasts and buried secrets to find love in the village of
Good Springs.

The Uncharted Beginnings Series
Embark on an unforgettable 1860s journey with the
Founders as they discover the Land.

Aboard Providence (#1)
When Marian and Jonah's ship gets marooned on a
mysterious uncharted island, they must build a settlement
to survive. Love and adventure await!

Above Rubies (#2)
When schoolteacher Olivia needs the settlement elders'
approval, she must hide her dyslexia from everyone, even
charming carpenter Gabe.

All Things Beautiful (#3)
Henry is the last person Hannah wants reading her
story… and the first person to awaken her heart.

Find out more on my website keelybrookekeith.com or
feel free to email me at keely@keelykeith.com where I
answer every message personally.

See you in the Land!
Keely

ABOUT THE AUTHOR

Keely Brooke Keith writes inspirational frontier-style fiction with a slight Sci-Fi twist, including *The Land Uncharted* (Shelf Unbound Notable Romance 2015) and *Aboard Providence* (2017 INSPY Awards Longlist).

Born in St. Joseph, Missouri, Keely was a tree-climbing, baseball-loving 80s kid. She grew up in a family who moved often, which fueled her dreams of faraway lands. When she isn't writing, Keely enjoys teaching home school lessons and playing bass guitar. Keely, her husband, and their daughter live on a hilltop south of Nashville, Tennessee.

For more information or to connect with Keely, visit her website www.keelybrookekeith.com.

Made in the USA
Middletown, DE
05 October 2023

40234248R00073